To Release an Earl

Ilene Withers

Clean Reads
www.CleanReads.com

I dedicate this book to three magnificent women:

my daughter, Lena Withers, for encouraging historical accuracy and helping me with plot ideas;

my mother, June Thompson, for reading my manuscripts and keeping up my self-esteem;

and Sarah Wernsing, my friend, confidant, and editor

Chapter One

Willa leaned forward in her saddle, relishing the wind in her face as it threatened to lift her velvet riding cap from her hair. The ground rushed by at an exhilarating speed as her horse's hooves flew over the landscape. There was no need to use a crop on her horse. Pirate was as excited about the opportunity to run as she was. A stone fence loomed ahead, and Willa encouraged her steed, "Let's take it, Pirate."

The distance between them and the fence diminished by the second, and they were soon upon it. As the horse lifted his front quarters from the ground, Willa heard a squawking from beneath them. Pirate jumped to the side as a bird flew from the shadows to hit his soft underbelly. Willa was barely cognizant of what was happening as her saddle left the horse's back. Suddenly sailing through midair, Willa realized she was free of the saddle and falling at an alarming speed toward the ground. Pain lanced through her body for a split second, as she made contact with the earth. Then her head snapped back and blackness enshrouded her.

John Herne, Earl of Roydon, dismounted his horse in front of his fiancée's home and climbed the few steps to the front door. He raised the knocker and greeted Abbott, Viscount Amhearst's aging butler.

"Abbott, how are you this fine day?" he greeted the man jovially.

"Fair enough, my lord." Abbott stepped back to allow John to step into the austere entry hall. The hall always struck John as being at complete odds with the family who lived there. He had grown quite fond of his future in-laws and knew them to be warm and genuine people.

"Is Miss Dutton in this afternoon?"

"Not at the moment, my lord. She is exercising her horse."

The butler's answer did not surprise John in the least. His beloved was an avid horsewoman; some might even call her horse mad. Willa had come by it honestly, for her father raised the finest blood stock in all of England.

A door to the right that John knew to be to the library opened and the viscount stepped into the hall. Yale Dutton hurried forward and extended his hand. "John," he greeted with enthusiasm, "I thought I heard your voice. Come on into the library so I can offer you a small restorative after your ride."

Before they had moved beyond the hallway, however, shouting made its way through the heavy oak door of the entrance.

"Help! Help!" It was a male voice, wrought with fear and worry.

Abbott hurried to the front door and pulled it open as John and Yale both rushed to step out. John felt his heart sink into his stomach when he recognized Brooks, Willa's groom, running his horse neck-or-nothing toward them. "Miss Dutton has had a terrible accident, my lord," the man uttered to the viscount. "The horse bucked her off, saddle and all. She flew over a fence and is lying at an odd angle, unconscious. Please come quick."

"Is she breathing, Brooks?" John asked, his stomach rolling and his chest feeling as though a giant claw had gripped it.

"She is, my lord. Her breaths are slow but steady. I draped my coat over her and left her lying, unsure what to do other than to fetch help. She's beyond the fence by the small pond."

The viscount shouted at his butler, "Have a groom bring me my horse and return the earl's horse. Have the stable hands hitch up a team to a flat wagon. Send someone for the physician with the utmost speed. Warn Lady Amhearst in the kindest way possible that Willa may be seriously injured."

Abbott hurried to do his master's bidding, and mere seconds passed before a groom returned with John's horse, having never left the yard before the alert had come. John swung himself onto the horse's back, trembling hands reaching for the reins. "Take me to her, Brooks." He glanced back at the viscount. "I'll hurry on ahead and see you as soon as you can get there." Then he reined his horse in behind the groom and urged the beast into the fastest gallop he could manage. During the short ride, he addressed the groom again. "What happened?"

"A bird flew up and hit Pirate in the belly just as he started to take the jump. The saddle and Miss Dutton both flew off his back. I don't know why, as I tightened the girth myself, my lord. I always double check it."

The groom dismounted at a gate and opened it for John. Once he had cleared the gate, John saw his beloved's crumpled figure. She lay at an odd angle over a slightly exposed tree root, her upper body twisted to the right from her lower body. John dreaded what he would find, but he needed to know. He leapt off his horse, dropping the reins, and hurried to her side.

John reached two fingers toward her neck, brushing aside the soft brown curls which had escaped her cap. He laid his fingers on her pulse. His hands were so unsteady he had to concentrate on holding them firm. At last he found it - a rhythmic one, two, three. Her pulse was sluggish but strong while her breathing was slow and even. Willa's skin was pale, yet warm to the touch.

The thundering of hooves announced the viscount's arrival along with another groom. "How is she?" the older man rasped as he slid from his saddle and hurried to his daughter's side. His skin was ashen and a pulsating vein stood out in his neck.

"She's alive," John replied. "Her pulse and her breathing are slow and steady, but I am worried about her possible injury. I have done a bit of reading on medicine, as you know, and I fear she may have a spinal injury due to the odd angle she is laying at. And when she fell she hit this tree root."

A sound of grief escaped the other man. "No," he keened, "not my Willa."

John looked up to see the viscount's face had contorted into pain. He stood up to grasp the viscount's shoulders as the man began to drop to his knees beside his daughter. "Listen, Yale," he spoke urgently, "from what little I know it is imperative we try not to move her more than necessary. The more forward thinking men of medicine have even stated it might be helpful to restrict the movements of someone who may have a spinal injury." Falling quiet for a few moments, John tried to remember all he had read about this. "I think we should send one of the grooms back to meet the wagon. Have them put together an unyielding stretcher of sorts. Do you have a door they can remove from its hinges?"

The viscount looked at John as though he were addlepated, before realization struck him. "Ah, I see," he said. "We would lift her carefully onto the door, keeping her spine as straight and immobile as possible to prevent further damage."

"Correct," John replied. "The wagon must drive as unhurriedly as possible along the smoothest route we can find."

With those words, the viscount looked at the second groom. "You heard the earl. Rush back to the stables and do whatever is necessary to put this together." As soon as the groom had galloped off, the viscount dropped down beside his daughter, tucking Brooks' coat around her still form with care.

John paced frantically, his breaths coming in bursts and gasps. He wanted to scream, yet he knew it would do nothing for the woman he loved. Instead, he forced himself to move and search for the saddle. Not seeing it, John realized it must be on the other side of the fence. "I'll be right back," he told the older man. He walked through the nearby gate and found the saddle lying in the tall grasses. As he picked it up, he noticed the leather of the girth had completely separated. After inspecting it, John swore it had been cut almost through from side to side just below the buckle. It was obvious to him from the remnants of frayed leather that the stress of the horse's movement had finished off the girth.

A nearby whinny directed his attention to Pirate, who had stayed close despite what must have been a fright for him. Brooks had approached the horse and was running his hands over the animal's legs and flank, inspecting him.

"Is Pirate injured?" John asked.

"He doesn't appear to be," the man replied. "He took a jump sideways, but landed alright."

John walked toward the groom and held out the saddle. "See the girth, Brooks."

The man rolled the leather over, ran his fingers and hands over it, and then grew pale. "It's been cut."

"Yes," John agreed, "but not completely. Just enough that the last bit frayed from the stress when Pirate jumped." John carried the saddle through the gate. Brooks and the horse followed.

"Yale, take a look at this saddle girth." John held it out toward the older man as he rose and approached.

The viscount inspected the saddle himself. "Someone has tampered with this," he said, his voice quiet. "This means someone attempted to and almost succeeded in killing my daughter. Why would anyone do this? And who is responsible?" He lifted his eyes to John's.

Before John could answer, the sound of a wagon and team could be heard in the distance. John laid the saddle down and moved back to kneel beside Willa, reaching out to stroke her cheek and once again check her pulse and breathing. His future father-in-law joined him.

"I hope they brought the door," the viscount said. "I think you are correct. We need to keep her as immobile as possible."

Both men raised their heads as riders approached followed by a wagon pulled by a team of two. They reined in their steeds and dismounted, soon reaching into the back of the wagon and pulling out a smooth wood door.

"Will this do, my lord?" a groom asked John and the viscount.

"That's exactly what I wanted," John praised the man. He then began to direct them. They would pad the door with one of the blankets they had brought along, then move it alongside her body. With as many hands on her as possible, they would gently slide her onto the board. Afterwards, they would use strips torn from another blanket to wrap around the door and Willa, firmly securing her to its ungiving surface.

John's heart raced and his hands shook despite his attempts to stay calm as all the men, including the viscount, looked to him for directions. It felt like an eternity before Willa laid on her back on the door, secured by narrow strips of wool. As he forced himself to take a deep and calming breath, John ordered the board be lifted in unison. They kept it parallel to the ground and carried it slowly to the back of the wagon without Willa rousing from her unconsciousness.

The drive back to the viscount's manor was tediously slow. Both John and Lord Amhearst rode next to Willa, wincing at every bump and rut they hit. They finally pulled up in front of the door. Lady Amhearst waited on the front step, pale and staring into the distance. Molly, Willa's maid, stood stalwart beside the viscountess as other household servants hovered nearby. As the wagon stopped, the small gathering surged forward to surround it.

John raised his head at the sound of an approaching vehicle to see a distinguished looking, middle-aged gentleman in a buggy pulled by a single horse. The viscount had become aware of the sound as well.

"Dr. Saunders," the older man greeted the newcomer as the buggy came to a halt near the wagon.

The doctor picked up his bag and jumped out of the vehicle, leaving the horse in the competent hands of a groom. "Tell me what happened, Lord Amhearst," the man ordered.

As the viscount recounted the unfortunate tale, John noticed the doctor's eyes often flickered toward Willa where she lay unconscious on the wooden door. At the end of the viscount's speech, the doctor approached the wagon. He climbed in and knelt beside Willa, checking her pulse, breathing, and opening each eyelid to look beneath. His hands ran over parts of her body – her legs and arms, hands and fingers. At last, he lifted his head to the people crowded around the wagon.

"It was wise to strap her to the door. Let's move her up to her room. We'll transfer her onto the bed with the blanket you've placed beneath her."

John took the lead, having a strong need to have his fiancée's life in his hands rather than someone else's. Abbott cleared the way, and Willa's mother and maid followed. The trip up the stairs to Willa's room was difficult, as they had to lift the bottom of the door to be even with the top of it. He had never been so thankful for wide stairways and hallways. Upon entering the room, the men found the covers rolled to the foot, leaving plenty of room to place Willa upon it without any impediment.

The physician hovered nearby, directing the movement of Willa from the door to the bed. When she was settled, the servants removed the door and binding strips from the room, the butler closing the door behind them. John, Molly, and the Amhearsts stayed behind and watched as Saunders unlaced Willa's boots and slid them from her feet. He then glanced at the maid and suggested she remove Willa's stockings. Although he politely averted his eyes as the maid did so, John soon found himself looking back at his beloved again.

Dr. Saunders opened his case and rummaged through the instruments within it. Extracting one, the physician approached the bed and ran it up Willa's bare foot from heel to toe. The man drew in a breath before speaking to them. "It's the slightest movement, but she moved her right foot a tiny bit. It's far too early to be sure, but most often someone who suffers from permanent paralysis has no reaction in their feet."

John exhaled, as did everyone in the room. She might not be paralyzed. Perhaps she would walk again, dance again, ride again. He knew just how much each of those activities meant to Willa. In fact, she had a vibrant personality which he feared would not adjust well to any permanent infirmity.

The doctor looked up at all of them, his eyes meeting each individual in the room. "I suggest you, Mrs. Amhearst, along with several maids, try to dress your daughter in a night rail with the slightest movement possible. All we can do at this point is make her as comfortable as possible and hope and pray for the best." He stepped over to search through his bag and retrieved a small bottle, which he pressed into Molly's hand. "Please alert me as soon as she wakes up and if she has pain give her six drops of this in a glass of water. However, unless she is suffering so much she cannot tolerate it, I would like it if you could hold off on the laudanum until I arrive."

John watched, his mind filled with too many questions to express, as Dr. Saunders lifted his bag and left the room. Yale Dutton glanced toward him, "Well, son, shall we leave the ladies alone to make Willa comfortable?"

"Yes," John replied with reluctance. "Would you like us to fetch the housekeeper?" he asked Willa's mother.

"Please do, John, and ask her to gather several maids to help Molly and me," Blythe Dutton said. She straightened her shoulders, the worry on her face replaced by a look of determination. "Have her bring several pairs of scissors. I believe we will cut the riding habit off to restrict the amount of movements we must make."

John and the viscount did not have to look far to locate Mrs. Bailey. She and many of the other servants clustered in the hall. It was Abbott who stepped forward toward his master. "How is she, my lord?"

The viscount nodded at the butler and then addressed the gathered servants. "We know nothing yet, other than she is unconscious and has a bit of feeling in her right foot. This should give us hope, but only time will tell. Until then, we will appreciate all of your prayers for our daughter. I fear she will need them."

Murmurs of, "Of course, my lord," "We will pray for her," and "Oh, poor Miss Willa," could be heard up and down the hall. It was John who walked over to the housekeeper, "Mrs. Bailey, could you ask the maids — perhaps at least six — to aid the viscountess, Molly, and yourself with changing Willa out of her clothing and into her night rail?"

The woman curtsied. "Yes, my lord." John nodded to his future father-in-law and moved toward the stairs. "I could use a drink, Yale."

Downstairs, the viscount led the way to the library where he poured a finger of scotch into two glasses. He walked across the room and handed one to John who took it with a nod of thanks. John lifted the glass to his lips. After letting the fiery liquid slide down his throat, John spoke to the older man.

"We have to find out what happened. The girth strap was cut!"

The viscount's hand visibly shook as he held the tumbler of liquor to his mouth. "Who would do this? Everyone loves our Willa."

"Yes, it is inconceivable."

John paced in front of the hearth, so many thoughts swirling through his mind that he couldn't keep his body still either. The viscount had slumped into a leather chair. Silence filled the room, interrupted only by the ticking of a clock and the occasional snap of an ember from the burning logs in the fireplace.

Half an hour passed before the door opened and Lady Amhearst appeared. "Willa is in her night rail. I have left her in Molly's care." John watched as the brave look on her face slipped and tears began to stream down her cheeks. The viscount stood and wrapped his strong arms around his wife and pulled her close.

Feeling *de trop*, John excused himself and stepped out of the library. In the entrance hall he encountered the butler. "Are my things in my usual room?" he asked Abbott, having stayed at the mansion a few times previously.

"They are, my lord, and your man arrived a few minutes ago. He is in your room, as well."

"Thank you, Abbott." John climbed the stairs. Turning to the left, he made his way through the guest wing to a west facing room decorated in masculine shades of dark green. He opened the door to find his valet, Martin, unpacking his valise. The other man turned at the sound of the door.

"I'm sorry, my lord. Is there any news about Miss Dutton yet?"

"Not much," John told his trusted and longtime servant. "She is unconscious, but the doctor did offer hope. When he ran an instrument up her feet, one of them twitched ever so slightly. Dr. Saunders insists people who are permanently paralyzed normally do not display even the slightest movement of the affected limbs."

"Well, that is something to hold onto," the valet replied.

"If you have everything you need," John began, "I'm going to wander out to the stables. I want to check on Pirate and speak to the stable master."

"Of course. Lord and Lady Amhearst's staff is exemplary and always welcoming. If I need anything, I shall ask."

With Martin's assurance, John left his room and then exited the house from the front door. The early fall air was most enjoyable; cooler than the oppressive heat of summer. Tree leaves were just beginning to shed their green and show a small amount of yellow in them. Flowers in the beds were looking a bit tired. Taking long, purposeful strides and calming deep breaths, John attempted to put aside his fear for Willa and focus on the tasks ahead. Whoever had cut the girth had meant her harm. Since it was her side saddle, the menace had been directed at her, not at anyone on the estate in general. John was sure the viscount had made, if not enemies, disgruntled acquaintances. After all, the man raised the best known stock in the equine industry. His horses fetched top dollar and won race after race. Competitions were his to command, which angered competitors.

At the stables, John walked through the open door past enclosures of livestock overlooking fenced green paddocks. He found Pirate in his stall with Brooks and another older man fussing over him.

"No lasting affects?" he enquired of the groom.

Both men raised their heads. "None I can see, my lord," the young groom assured John. "Far less than his mistress has experienced." His voice was filled with concern.

John squeezed his eyes shut for a moment against the vivid image of Willa lying twisted across the tree root. The knowledge of how close her head had come to the trunk of the tree sent a shiver down his spine. He opened his eyes and directed them to the older man. "You're the stable master, aren't you?"

"Yes, my lord. My name's Ward."

"Did Brooks tell you about the girth strap on Miss Dutton's saddle being cut?"

"He did, my lord. I have already spoken to all the men about it. No one claims to have any knowledge about what happened. I believe each should be questioned in private, though. 'Specially in light of the other incidents," the other man finished.

Chapter Two

"Pray tell, what other incidents do you mean?" John asked the stable master.

"There's been several times something has happened that is a bit fishy. Couple weeks ago, the viscount and Miss Willa were out riding, and the viscount got bucked off his horse. Didn't hurt him none 'cause he landed in the pond. Ruined a fine pair of boots, though."

"Hmm."

"One of the grooms was along and told me later in confidence he saw something fly out of a nearby bush and hit the horse in the flank."

"Did he say what it was?"

"He wasn't sure, my lord, but said it looked like nothin' more than a rock. It came out of the bush pretty hard, though. Like a slingshot might have been used." Ward stopped and chewed on his lower lip.

"Anything else?" John prompted the man to continue.

"Miss Willa's bridle was damaged. The tack boy caught it and showed me. The leather looked like it had been worn through, like mebbe someone had used a file."

"Was it just those two incidents?" John asked.

"No. There's more. Pirate was actin' skittish a few weeks back. That's unusual. I noticed it right away and wondered if he had gotten into something."

John thought about this a moment. "What do you mean by skittish?" he asked the older man.

"Pirate's gait was off, and he twitched his legs. Fact is, he acted nervous," Ward replied. "I saw Miss Marty in the village the next day and spoke to her about it. She said it sounded like lupine."

"Lupine," John said on an exhaled breath. "We once had a colt which got into lupine and acted the same way."

The stable master nodded. "There's lupine grows down by the pond but the horses aren't allowed to graze there. And usually, a horse won't eat poisonous plants. They seem to know better."

"Not if it's ground up and mixed with other feed, such as oats," John mused. "Who is Miss Marty?" he asked after a moment, remembering the name Ward had mentioned.

"She's the daughter of the Baron Townsend," Ward started. "Well, he's passed on, and her brother is the baron now. Anyways, Miss Marty has a way with animals, particularly farm animals."

"Interesting," John replied, surprised a woman would be known for her knowledge of farm animals, especially the daughter of a peer. "Did you tell the viscount of your misgivings, Ward?" he asked the stable master, returning to the problem at hand.

"I did. He was concerned about Pirate's behavior, but the horse worked it out of his system within a few days like Miss Marty told me he would. Otherwise, the master more or less dismissed the problems. You know how he is, though. He's a good and trusting man."

"That he is," John agreed. "He thinks the best of everyone."

Ward regarded him as though seeking direction. John spoke again. "I'm going to speak to Lord Amhearst about these incidents again. In the meantime, please be extra vigilant around the stables. If I can get permission from Lord Amhearst to do so, I'll start to speak to each of the men who work in the stables or has access to the horses."

"That'd be a good idea," Ward agreed. "If it comes from you, they might take it seriously, too. And I will keep an eye out on things."

John nodded and then began to walk back to the house.

❧

Willa woke slowly. She became aware of the darkness in the room and lifted her eyelids. Her head ached and she had a dreadful pain in her back, slightly above her waist. As she squeezed her eyes shut against it, she concentrated on taking slow deep breaths to ease the hurt. It didn't help, and she realized she was sleeping on her back, which might have been the problem. Normally, she slept on one side or the other. Now, twisting her upper torso, she tried to roll over by swinging one leg over the other as usual.

Her leg wouldn't move! It just lay there, heavy against the mattress. Willa tried again, and it still would not move. The pain in her back increased. A sense of panic slipped in, overwhelming her, and she twisted her head from side to side before Molly leaned over her.

"Shh, Miss Willa. You've been injured. Try to lie still."

Willa stared at her dear maid. "Injured?"

"Yes, Miss. You were bucked off your horse."

"Please light a candle, Molly," Willa begged, trying to make sense of her maid's words. She waited until she heard the strike of the flint and a growing flame lit a circle of light near the bed. "Now, please tell me again."

"I will," Molly assured her, "but first I must let someone know to fetch the doctor. He wanted to be alerted as soon as you woke. There's a footman outside the door, so I'll only be a moment."

Willa watched as the maid walked to the door and spoke in hushed tones Willa was unable to make out. Then Molly returned to her side.

"You were bucked off your horse, Miss Willa. Brooks saw it happen and came back to fetch help. He said you landed hard on an exposed tree root."

Willa strained to remember anything of the incident. Her head ached enough to make concentration difficult. She had little time to think before her bedroom door swung open and her parents, followed by her fiancé stepped into the room, all swathed in dressing gowns.

"Willa, darling," her mother said as she hurried to the bedside, "you're awake."

Willa's mouth was dry as she glanced from one to the other of the three people she loved most in the world. "Molly said Pirate bucked me off."

"It's true," her father said. "Brooks said a bird flew up and hit Pirate's belly just before you took the fence."

"Is Pirate okay?" she asked, worried about her beloved dark bay.

This time John stepped closer and reached for her hand in the dimness, squeezing it gently as he grasped it in his own. "Pirate is fine," he assured her. "Brooks and Ward have both been over him multiple times."

"I can't believe he unseated me," she replied. "He's been hit by birds in the past. Why last year, a duck reared out of the rushes and hit him in the lower left flank. Pirate jumped sideways at least three yards, and I stayed on him." As she spoke, she noticed her father open his mouth to speak, but John cleared his throat. John caught her father's eye, and he shook his head ever so slightly. Willa narrowed her eyes. What were they signaling to each other?

A soft knock sounded at the door, and Molly hurried to open it. She spoke again in hushed tones, and then turned back to the room. "Dr. Saunders has been sent for, my lords and lady."

"Thank you, Molly," the viscountess said. Blythe returned her attention to her daughter and reached out to stroke Willa's brunette hair out of her face. "What can we do to make you more comfortable, dear?"

"May I have something to drink?" she asked.

"Of course, whatever you want," came the reply.

"How about a nice cup of tea?" Molly suggested.

Willa nodded as her maid hurried away to once again speak to the footman in the hall. "Why can't I move my legs?" Willa asked her loved ones. "And why does my back hurt so?" She watched as her parents both shifted their eyes away from her. Next, she let her gaze land on John's face. He seemed uncomfortable but didn't look away. Love and concern showed in his blue eyes.

"It's too early to know," he told her as he took her hand and rubbed the pad of his thumb over the back of hers. "Dr. Saunders will be able to explain more when he arrives. How bad is the pain in your back?" he asked.

"It hurts, but is not unbearable," she answered.

"The doctor left laudanum for you," her mother told her. "However, he said he would rather you not use it until he has seen you, unless you are in much pain."

"No," Willa assured her. "I'll be okay. Mostly, I'm scared," she whispered. "I want to know why I can't move my legs." When the others remained quiet and looked away from her eyes, she grew more determined and more frightened. "Its paralysis, isn't it?"

"We can't know for sure," John told her. "The doctor will arrive soon, and we should leave your diagnosis up to him." The door opened and a footman stepped inside with a tea tray. "Ah, look," her fiancé said, "your tea has arrived."

Molly took the tray and set it on the bedside table. She poured the beverage into a delicate china cup before looking at Willa's mother. "Should I raise her head with more pillows?"

"I believe it would be acceptable," the viscountess replied.

John offered to help, and he carefully slid his hands under her head and shoulders, lifting them from the mattress as the maid put two more feather pillows beneath Willa's head. Molly handed her the cup of tea and hurried to light more candles. Willa took a sip of the hot liquid and savoured it. She pondered about what it would be like if she could never move her legs again. Trying to be an optimist, she spoke again.

"At least I can move my arms," she said. Willa held the cup and saucer in her left hand so she experimentally moved her right arm up into the air, over to the side, and then out in front of her. She switched the cup into her other hand and repeated the movement with her left arm. "I have a full range of motion," she stated with false bravado. Inside, though, she felt none of it.

She noticed her parents and John seemed uncomfortable. Her father fetched a chair for her mother and insisted she sit. Willa watched them, wanting them to fill the silence with chatter which would take her mind off her injury. Thinking about her legs, she tried to move them. Finally, to quit worrying, she asked about her horse once more. "You're sure Pirate is not injured? You would tell me if he was, wouldn't you?" Noticing a shrill edge of panic in her voice, Willa tried to calm herself.

John perched on the edge of the bed, took the cup and saucer from her hand and passed it to Molly. Then he grasped both of Willa's hands in his. "Pirate is fine, although he seems to sense something is wrong. It is as if he knows you have been hurt and he feels at fault."

A quiet knock sounded at the door at last and Molly rushed to open it, ushering in Dr. Saunders. "Well, Miss Willa, I am glad to see you are awake," the physician said.

Willa thought a moment about having been bucked off and then replied quietly, "Yes, I might have been killed, mightn't I?"

"It is true," the doctor said. "Many people aren't so lucky." He regarded those gathered in the room, "Why don't you all step into the hall, except for Molly, of course?"

They seemed hesitant, Willa thought, but finally her parents and John obeyed the doctor's suggestion. The doctor sat down his bag and asked Molly to pull back the covers before proceeding to tap each of her knee caps. Willa felt nothing. He took out a sharp instrument and ran it up the bottom of her bare right foot.

"That tickles!" Willa tried to jerk her foot away and couldn't.

"You felt it?" he asked her.

"I did and it tickled, but I tried to move my foot away from it, and I could not."

He repeated it on her left foot. Willa prepared herself for the same reaction, but it did not come.

"I assume you did not feel it this time?"

Willa shook her head, "No."

"Your right foot did twitch somewhat, although you did not feel you could move it. The tiny movement is a good sign."

The doctor proceeded to check her pulse and her breathing, inspected her eyes as he moved a candle back and forth in front of her face. He picked up her arms and rotated them. "Now, tell me where you are experiencing pain," he commanded.

"In my back, above my waist."

"Is it in the center, or to one side or the other?"

Willa closed her eyes and concentrated on her back pain. "A bit to the left of center," she answered.

"And you can't move your legs or feet no matter how hard you concentrate?"

Willa tried again, grimacing with concentrated effort. "No, Doctor, I cannot," she said, not trying to hide the disappointment in her voice.

"And does your head ache?"

"A bit," she admitted.

"You took an extremely serious fall," the man told her. "It's my understanding you landed hard on an exposed tree root. Lord Roydon said you were lying on the tree root at about the location your back hurts." He paused and then moved on with seeming determination. "I'll not mince words, Miss Willa. I believe your spine has been injured. The twitching in your foot and the sensation in your right lower limb give me hope you will someday walk again, but I cannot promise it. You may well be suffering from paralysis from the waist down for the rest of your life. I know it is terribly difficult, but I recommend you try to come to terms with the possibility."

Willa sighed and spoke her fears in a wavering voice. "I was afraid of that." She despised the tears which slipped unbidden down her cheeks.

"I will speak to your father about obtaining a Bath chair for you. Perhaps he could purchase one for each floor as you improve. A footman could carry you between stairs, and this wheeled chair will keep you from being confined to your room or even to the house. With a bit of ingenuity, all kinds of accommodations can be made for a Bath chair."

"I'm to get married this winter," she said.

"You might want to postpone your nuptials until you recover more," the doctor suggested. "It would not be wise to risk having a child at this time," he continued.

More tears slid down her cheek. "I understand," she murmured as an ache settled in her chest.

She watched through a film of moisture as the doctor tucked his instruments back into his bag. He picked the bag up and looked back at Willa. "Your maid has laudanum she can give you if you would like to take it to dull the pain. And I'll be back tomorrow to check on you."

"Molly," Willa called to her maid as the other young woman was escorting the doctor to the door, "please tell my parents and the earl I am tired and wish to be alone now."

"Yes, miss," Molly said, "but I will stay with you if you should need anything."

Willa wished to dismiss her but recognized how dependent she would now be on others. Why, she couldn't even use a chamber pot.

Chapter Three

John could have indulged himself by sleeping late, but the truth was he couldn't sleep. Worry over Willa had kept him awake. Memories of this past summer when John had traveled to London to take part in the season with his best friend, Noel Mallory, the Duke of Lamberton, filled his thoughts. Noel had immediately met Miss Claire Stuart who had captured his heart. Miss Stuart, had displayed some bizarre behavior owing to the secret of being blackmailed by Miss Regina Norton, a woman John's late father had wished for him to marry. Miss Norton, it was discovered, had blackmailed Miss Stuart into trying to capture John's hand in marriage so she might marry another. Yet even before the discovery of the blackmail plot, John had met Claire's cousin, Miss Willa Dutton. The two were thrown together often during the season at social events in their efforts to smooth the way for Noel and Claire. Upon meeting Willa, John had admired her spirit and beauty, and it didn't take long for admiration to become love.

John had never expected to make a love match, and he felt luckier than any man should be to know he would live the rest of his life with Willa at his side. Now their wedding was set for mere weeks away over the holidays. Claire and Noel had married a few weeks earlier and traveled to the continent to enjoy a lengthy honeymoon in Paris and Salzburg before returning to their palatial estate not far from John's own home.

Somehow knowing his employer was no longer asleep, Martin slipped into the room with a pot of coffee. He set the tray on a table and approached the bed, reaching for John's dressing gown. Discreetly looking the other way, he held up the robe and waited as John slipped out of bed and into the garment.

"Did you sleep well, my lord?"

"No," John replied frankly. "The night was fraught with worry over my fiancée."

"The entire household is worried about Miss Willa, as they all fondly call her. I believe everyone is praying to the Lord to heal her."

"It is appreciated," John said. "Willa woke in the night and realized she cannot move her legs. Lord and Lady Amhearst and I tried not to say much to her, but I am sure she was suspicious. She has not been bucked off a horse since learning to ride as a child, and she seemed to be scared, although facing it as well as can be expected."

"I heard the physician was called."

"He was, and he examined her and then came out to tell us he told her we must all wait and see. She still has some feeling in one of her lower limbs and a small reaction, although she cannot move them. We were ready to go back in when her maid told us she wished to be alone."

"It must be a lot to absorb," Martin murmured as he poured a cup of coffee, added a touch of cream and a cube of sugar, and handed it to the earl. "What will you be wishing to wear today?"

"Please choose for me," John told his trusted man. "I intend to visit Willa and spend a bit of time at the scene of her accident and in the stable talking to the staff."

Less than an hour later, John emerged from his room, freshly shaven and dressed in a bottle green jacket, brown breeches, and polished Hessians. Making his way down the stairs to the dining room, John found his future father-in-law breaking his fast. The older man looked up as John entered the room.

"You look like you slept even less than I did, John."

"It's true I slept little, and what brief times I did sleep were troubled with worry." Though not hungry, he forced himself to cross to the buffet and dish up a coddled egg, a rasher of bacon, and a toasted muffin before sitting next to the viscount.

"I am going to ride out to the site of the accident today," he told Lord Amhearst. "I'd like to see if there are any tracks anywhere near, if I can find a nest where the bird flew up, or if it might have been released in the same location as where Willa approached the fence."

"May I ride out with you?" Yale asked him. "I can't sit here wondering and worrying. It would feel good to take some action."

"Yes, and afterwards I would like to question the stable staff. Ward suggested each employee be questioned in private. Would you give me permission to do so?"

"Even better, I'll join you in the questioning."

"Do you know how Willa is doing this morning? I'm worried about her – not just physically, but also mentally."

"I sought out Molly in the kitchen," the viscount said. "The maid had been awake most of the night so was quite tired and turning over her duties to another maid. Willa was quiet except for occasional sobbing. Molly did tell me Dr. Saunders told Willa she should consider postponing the wedding as she dare not risk getting with child until she knows more about her condition."

John swore under his breath. Hearing the news must have broken Willa's heart. She had been planning their wedding ceremony with enthusiasm and had often spoken about how she could not wait to provide John with an heir to the earldom. "We'll be able to buy a small pony for our child, John," she had said not long ago. He knew his fiancée was anxious to become a mother. To postpone their wedding and delay having a family could throw her into a deep depression.

"I'm going to talk to Blythe about hiring another personal maid for Willa," Yale said after a moment or two of silence. "Molly won't be able to handle the demands on her time."

"I agree," John said. "It is important Willa have continual care. After all, she cannot do much of anything for herself now."

The two men were quiet as they finished their morning meal, each lost in his own thoughts. As they drank their last sips of the now lukewarm coffee, Yale looked over at John. "Let us go get our mounts and ride out to investigate the area where the accident happened."

Half an hour later, the two men were walking slowly around the area where Pirate had bucked off his mistress. John found the hoof prints where the horse had jumped several feet to the side after the bird must have hit him in the belly. He squatted down and brushed aside the tall grasses to examine the ground but found no tracks of a human being near the area. Neither was there any bird's nest.

"Well," he addressed the viscount, "I haven't found anything suspicious here."

"Neither have I," the older man said. "Shall we ride back to the stables and question the grooms and stable workers?"

"Yes," John said as he walked over to collect his tethered horse. After mounting and settling into his saddle he addressed the viscount. "Ward told me you were bucked off recently."

"Indeed! I landed in the pond and got thoroughly drenched, but I came to no other harm."

"Ward told me the groom saw your horse was hit with something."

"Yes," Lord Amhearst stated. "Ford, my groom, said it appeared to be a rock. The man said it came flying out of a bush with quite a bit of force."

"Was Willa with you?"

"She was." Yale laughed, "In fact, it was the same moment she challenged me to a race and flew past me."

"Any chance the rock was meant to hit her horse instead of yours?"

The viscount grew thoughtful. When he spoke again, his voice was filled with emotion. "Now when you ask me about it, she was closer to the bush Ford said it came out of than I was. Perhaps it was meant for Pirate. If a slingshot had been used, it might have already been shot when she raced past me. In fact, I suspect she was about a stride ahead of me when the rock hit my horse's flank."

"Ward told me her bridle had been cut through as well, but the tack boy caught it."

"Yes, I do remember him mentioning something about it. I assumed it was worn."

"And the lupine?" John asked.

The older man looked at him sharply. "Lupine?"

"When Pirate was behaving skittishly," John prodded. "I talked to Ward about it. He said a local baron's daughter said the symptoms have all the markings of lupine poisoning. Apparently, she is well versed in animal care."

The viscount swore under his breath. "And I dismissed it," he said. Yale turned moist eyes to John. "Someone is trying to kill my little girl, aren't they?"

"I'm afraid there's a good chance of it," John replied, feeling sick at the thought.

❧

Willa had spent a fretful night. Her heart was heavy. Dr. Saunders had told her to postpone her wedding and how she dare not risk becoming pregnant in her condition. Willa ached to be a mother, to give John an heir. The thought of being unable to do so broke her heart.

Molly had stayed with her during the night. Willa doubted her maid had slept at all, for she had been at the bedside to wipe Willa's face dry of tears, to whisper comforting words, and to fluff the pillows. The maid deserved a thank you, but Willa was so overwrought she wasn't sure she could form the words.

At dawn, Molly had opened the door to allow in another maid, her mother's Luvina. The two women exchanged a few whispered words before Molly slipped out the door and Luvina appeared at Willa's bedside. Within a few minutes, a pot of hot tea had been delivered to the room, and the middle-aged maid encouraged Willa to have a cup of it.

"You must drink, Miss Willa, and you need to eat breakfast as well. Cook has promised to fix whatever you'd like to tempt your appetite."

Willa shook her head. "I'm not hungry," she whispered.

Luvina smoothed back Willa's hair. "I understand, miss, but you must keep up your strength. The doctor said he holds hope for you. Keep it in mind."

Willa closed her eyes and tried to focus on the maid's words. Hope. Dr. Saunders had said he had hope. Could she dig deep enough inside herself to find her own hope?

"Maybe a soft boiled egg and a slice of toast," she said at last. "And could you help me sit up a bit more so I can drink the tea?"

Luvina rewarded her with a broad smile. "Of course. Let me just fetch two more pillows."

A few minutes later, Willa was reclining against the pillows and sipping her tea. Luvina had tugged the bell pull and ordered the meal Willa had suggested. She had drunk about half her tea when the bed chamber door opened and her mother entered.

"Good morning, dear," the viscountess said cheerfully.

"Morning." Willa replied, unable to add a "good" to the greeting. She watched as her mother approached the bed and seemed to nervously hover over her. Then her mother fluffed the pillows, smoothed Willa's hair, and straightened the bed covers.

"How are you this morning?" she asked.

"I can't move my legs," Willa answered bluntly, feeling like a petulant child. "It doesn't matter how hard I try. I can't!"

Her mother seemed to ignore Willa's proclamation. "And the pain you had in your back?" she asked instead.

"Is still there."

"Did Molly give you any laudanum?"

"She offered it to me, and I refused it. I have always hated how it effects me. Remember when you made me take it when I sprained my ankle?"

"I do, but if the pain becomes unbearable, promise me you will take it," the viscountess pleaded.

Willa nodded her promise.

"Perhaps willow bark tea would help, Miss Willa," Luvina interrupted with the offer.

"What a good idea," Lady Amhearst said. "Would the tea be so objectionable?" she asked her daughter.

"No," Willa said, "after I've eaten, I would be willing to drink it."

The door opened, and a young kitchen maid appeared with a tray. She approached the bed and set the tray over Willa's lap. Then she bobbed a curtsy and left the room without saying a word.

The tray held a plate with hearty toast, a small dish of jam, an egg cup with a soft-boiled egg, and a vase with a sunny yellow rose which must have been cut in the greenhouse. Willa reached up and caressed one soft petal. "I wish I could see Claire," she said to her mother, speaking of her favorite cousin and best friend, who was now the new Duchess of Lamberton and a gardening enthusiast.

"I understand, dear," the viscountess said. Luvina placed a chair behind the older woman and Willa's mother perched on the edge of the seat. "I have already alerted your aunt and uncle of your accident, but you wouldn't want to interrupt your cousin's wedding trip, would you?"

"No," Willa whispered as she spread jam thick on the piece of toast and bit into it. Chewing slowly, she tried to find enjoyment in the taste of the crunchy bread and its sweet topping. Unfortunately, the toast seemed dry in her mouth, and she laid it back on the plate. "I'm not hungry," she said as she took one final sip of her tea. "Please," she turned to implore Luvina, "take the tray away." Then she looked at her mother, "I didn't sleep well last night, and I'm tired. I am going to take a nap now."

John suggested Lord Amhearst take the seat behind the stable master's desk in the man's small office. He then went out to collect the first man they wanted to speak with. Approaching Willa's groom, John asked him to step into the office.

"Have a seat, Brooks," the viscount said. "Lord Roydon and I would like you to tell us everything you remember about the events of yesterday."

Brooks looked the viscount in the eye and then shifted his glance to look straight into John's eyes and back to his employer's. "Miss Willa came out in the early afternoon, about two I guess, and asked me to saddle Pirate. I did, and saddled a horse for myself as well. The girth was snug, but I didn't inspect the underside of it where it had been cut. My lady told me to expect a fast ride. We left the stables and rode east as we usually do. As soon as we cleared the yard, she urged Pirate into a fast gallop. Everything seemed fine until we approached the fence." The groom stopped and cleared his throat, shifting in his chair, moving his gaze to meet John's.

"Go on," John encouraged him.

Brooks nodded and continued. "Just as Pirate lifted his front hooves from the ground, a bird flew up from the grass. It may have been a grouse which hit him right in the belly. The horse was spooked. He jumped to the left about three feet, bucking as he did it. When his legs hit the ground, Miss Willa flew off his back. It was the oddest thing, she was still sittin' on the side saddle. Then she went over the fence and the saddle fell on this side of it." The man tapered off and then reached up to wipe at his eyes.

It was obvious to John how much the man cared about Willa. Yale was scribbling notes in a book and paused long enough to look up. "Thank you, Brooks. It's just the information we are needing."

"Is she going to be alright?" he asked the men.

His employer answered him. "We don't know much," Yale said. "The doctor has said there is some hope she may not permanently suffer from paralysis. It will take time to tell if she'll ever ride Pirate again. I'm thankful she's alive."

"Yes, my lord. I feared I would not find her so."

John waited a few moments before asking another question. "Tell us what else you have noticed – anything which comes to mind which seems suspicious, strangers who might have been in the vicinity of the stables."

The groom was quiet and thoughtful. "I heard Ward tell you about Pirate acting skittish," he addressed John.

"Yes, we talked about how it sounded like lupine."

"That's right. I don't have any idea how it got in his food if that is what happened. Then there was the time Miss Willa's bridle was cut. The tack boy brought it to my attention, and I took it to Ward."

"Have there been any strangers around the stables?" John asked Brooks.

Brooks looked at the viscount and then back at John. "There's always strangers around the stables. Lord Amhearst here has gentlemen coming in most days. They want to tour the stables and inspect the stock. Most of them prob'ly can't afford to buy, but they want to think about it."

"You're right, Brooks. The viscount has a sterling reputation, doesn't he?"

"The best, my lord. It's an honor to work here."

"Is there any one visitor who stands out more than the others? Someone who has visited more than once or been around not long before each of the incidents?" John inquired.

The groom was quiet for several minutes, seeming deep in thought. At last, he shook his head, "No, my lord, none I can think of."

Yale thanked the young man and asked him to send the tack boy into the office. When the gangly, freckle faced boy entered the room, the viscount invited him to sit on the empty chair. "Jem, I'm sure you remember Lord Roydon, Miss Willa's fiancé."

The boy looked at John and nodded, an action which made him seem older than what John estimated to be about fourteen years of age. "My lord," he said.

"Thank you for joining us, Jem," John said, hoping to put the boy at ease. "I'm sure you've heard about Miss Willa's accident yesterday."

"Of course. I heard it was bad. We're all worried about her."

"As are we," the viscount said. "We're trying to get an idea as to whether or not someone might have wanted to bring her harm."

The boy looked up at the two men earnestly. "Why would anyone want to hurt Miss Willa?"

"We don't know," the viscount replied. "It does seem nonsensical. Can you think of anyone who would have a reason to or who has been acting suspiciously?"

"No, my lord," Jem answered. "O'course there's always strangers around, but no one I can think of who's been back again or been where they shouldna' ha' been."

"Tell us about when you found out the bridle had been tampered with," John prodded.

"'Bout a month ago, I noticed Pirate's bridle was hanging on the wrong hook. I figured someone had gotten sloppy, but when I picked it up, I saw the headpiece had been most cut through. Like someone had used a file or a knife to cut through but not quite all the way. If I hadn't a caught it, it could ha' busted when she was running hard, and she could ha' lost control of the horse."

"And you brought it to Ward's attention?" John asked

"Yes. He asked around about it, but no one claimed to know anything. Afterwards, I started payin' more attention to who went in there. I guess I didn't do good enough, though, if her girth strap was cut the same way."

John noticed Jem's scowl and clenched jaw. Jem was angry at the thought. Again, he didn't think this young man would cause any harm to Willa but someone had, and John felt he needed to look at everyone as a possible suspect.

"Who all has access to the tack room?" he asked the boy.

"Everyone," was the reply. "I don't never see no strangers go in," he went on, "but Ward and all the grooms use it regular like."

"Can you think of anything else important to tell us?" Lord Amhearst asked him.

The young man shook his head and then rose to go after the viscount thanked him. As he got to the door, he turned. "If there's anything I can do for Miss Willa, I'll do it. She's a bang-up lady."

The afternoon stretched on as John and Yale interviewed each stable employee down to the young boy who mucked out the stalls. All the answers were similar – no one had seen anyone unusual around except for the strangers who were in and out on an almost daily basis. Each expressed concern, and several seemed genuinely distraught.

At the end of the day, John ran a hand through his hair. "I don't feel we made any headway," he told the older man. "To be honest, I am even more frustrated."

"I know, son," the viscount said as he laid a comforting hand on John's shoulder. "I understand how you are feeling."

"I think I'll wash up and get the stable odor off me, then change and visit Willa," he told the viscount.

"Can I make a suggestion?"

"Of course."

"Go the way you are. My daughter will find the smells of the stable comforting."

Chapter Four

Willa was feigning sleep when there was a tapping at the door. Luvina rose from the chair next to the bed and walked across the room to answer the summons. John's voice, albeit quiet, could be heard.

"How is she?"

"She's resting, my lord," the maid replied.

"Would you mind if I came in for a few moments? I would like to check on her."

"Certainly."

Willa peeped from beneath her lashes to see the man she loved walk across the room until he loomed at the side of the bed.

"I know you're awake, Willa." John's voice was tinged with the sound of amusement.

Willa sighed and opened her eyes to search his handsome face. She noticed his dark brown hair was mussed as though he had run his fingers through it in frustration. His blue eyes were troubled, and he smelled of horse, an odor Willa loved.

"You've been in the stables," she stated. "How is Pirate?"

"Your stallion is no worse for the wear," John replied, "but he misses you and seems to sense something is wrong."

"No doubt. Pirate's an intelligent horse." Willa fell silent then. Her fiancé reached out a hand and stroked her brow, letting his fingers brush her cheek as he raised his hand. Willa leaned her face into his touch, taking comfort from it.

"Tell me the truth, John," Willa begged. "Am I suffering from paralysis?"

Willa watched as he seemed to gauge his words. "Your spine appears to be injured," he said at last. "Whether it means you are permanently paralyzed is a question Dr. Saunders cannot answer at this time. There is some feeling in your right foot. This is a reason to give us all hope."

"But I cannot move my legs. Even when I concentrate on it, nothing happens. Even the slightest movement is not possible for me to make."

"Right now," John said. "You can't move them right now. Remember, we do not know what the future holds."

"The doctor said we need to postpone our wedding," she said with a quiver in her voice. "He said I cannot risk having a child in this condition."

"There's still time. Let us not worry about our nuptials now."

John looked around the room and then at the maid. "It's Luvina, correct?"

"Yes, my lord."

"Why don't you open the draperies, Luvina?"

"Of course, my lord." The maid hustled to do as she was bid.

"I was trying to rest," Willa said.

"You love the outdoors," John reminded her, "and a dark room is depressing. It's more important now than ever for you to have the cheerful sunshine in your room. Besides, my love, I like to see your beautiful face in better light than this dimness."

"Humph," Willa snorted, crossing her arms across her chest. She was not feeling cheerful, and she wanted to surround herself with darkness. "I'd rather they be closed."

"Too bad," John replied. "In fact, now that I can see again, why don't I go fetch a book and read aloud to you? Or we could play chess or cards. Otherwise, since it is almost time for luncheon, I could have mine brought up as well and I could eat with you."

"Would you like me to ring for luncheon?" Luvina put in. "Miss Willa didn't eat her breakfast, so she must be hungry."

"I'm not," Willa spoke crossly at the same time as John said, "Please do, Luvina."

He looked around while the maid walked to the door. Finding the chair Lady Amhearst had occupied, John pulled it up to the bedside.

"I hope I don't reek too much of horse."

"Would you go change if I said you did?" Willa asked. She loved him, but he was grating on her nerves being as cheerful as he was. She was usually a cheerful person herself, but all she wanted to do now was cry in solitude.

He just grinned and replied, "No, you love the smell of the stables and I want to make sure you eat your luncheon."

"Well, you can't force it down my throat," she said, staring down at her arms. She felt like throwing a temper tantrum. Oh, how she wanted her legs back!

"Ah, is this the book you've been reading?" he asked as she heard him pick up the bound copy from the bedside table. "*Sense and Sensibility* by Jane Austen," he read. "I've heard about this novel. In fact, my mother told me not long ago she was going to purchase it at the first opportunity."

"I've barely started it," Willa mumbled, looking up at him out of curiosity despite her bad mood.

"I'm glad. This way we can start it over together, and I'll read it to you each day. It will be our book." With that stated, he removed the bookmark, flipped back to the first page, and began to read. "'The family of Dashwood had long been settled in Sussex.'"

"You won't be interested in this, John," Willa interrupted in her wish to be left alone in her misery.

"We're going to be man and wife, dear. This means we should share many interests. 'Their estate was large, and their residence was at Norland Park,'" he went on.

Willa gave up and let herself be lost in the sound of his rich, masculine voice as he read the words of the new novel to her. She watched his face as he read, finding the emotions flitting across it as he read to be fascinating. John did not pause until lunch arrived.

❧

After a luncheon of meat pies, cheese, and fresh fruit during which John begged and cajoled Willa to eat, he read to her from the Austen book until her eyelids drooped into slumber. Then, laying the book on the bedside table and rising to brush a tender kiss across Willa's forehead, he nodded to the maid and slipped out of the room.

Once the door was shut, he leaned against the wall, exhausted and angry. He wasn't angry at Willa but at some unknown foe who had intentionally battered his beloved both physically and mentally. His usually lighthearted and fun-loving fiancée was depressed and scared and bitter. He couldn't blame her. In her circumstances, he would have been, too.

He walked down the stairs and found his host and hostess ensconced in the library looking worried. Blythe was chewing her bottom lip, and the viscount was tapping his fingers on his desk. They looked up as he walked into the room.

"How is she, John?" her mother asked.

"Depressed and scared," he answered truthfully. "I asked the maid to open the draperies and let the sunlight in. Then I read to her from her book and persuaded her to eat most of her lunch. She fought me almost every step of the way."

"But you did get her to eat?" Yale asked.

"Yes, most of it. She also listened to the book as I read aloud. By the time I left she had fallen asleep."

"Molly said she laid awake most of the night, often sobbing relentlessly," Blythe said. "My heart aches for my darling little girl."

"Ours all do," her husband put in. "You said earlier she told you she missed Claire. Maybe we should see if Fayre would come to visit. What is she, eighteen now?"

"A year younger, dear," Blythe returned, "but it is an excellent idea. Fayre is such a sweet girl."

John knew they were talking about Willa's cousin, Claire's younger sister. "I think the distraction would be a good idea." John paused before saying to Yale, "And you mentioned you were going to hire another maid to help Molly with Willa's care."

"Yes, I've already talked to Abbott about seeking a nurse for her. He suggested an employment agency in Bath where we might find more nurses than we would at other places. In fact, he has already sent one of the grooms to Bath with a request and an order for two Bath chairs as Dr. Saunders suggested."

"That will be helpful," John said. "The mobility to leave her room will be good for her."

The viscountess rose and made her excuses. "You are correct, John, and so I am going to go write a letter to my sister begging she send Fayre."

"They will be happy to," her husband told her. "Let us ask Abbott to arrange for a carriage to deliver the request and return with Fayre. Perhaps we can send one of the parlour maids along to serve as a chaperone for her."

John sank into the chair his future mother-in-law had abandoned and regarded the viscount across the desk. "Is there anyone we should question? Anyone we haven't yet spoken to?"

"Of course, we could speak to the household staff," Yale said, "but I'm reluctant to. Gossip has a way of making its way around the house, and I don't want to worry Willa with our fears."

"I agree," John said. "She's already scared enough."

"I will speak to the butler and housekeeper in confidence, however. Both can be trusted not to say anything to anyone else but can then keep their eyes and ears open for anything which may be suspicious and report it back to me."

John was quiet a moment before standing up again. "I cannot stand still until we get this figured out," he said. "I'll go back out to the stables. Everything seems to lead to there. At least I'll feel like I'm doing something."

He left the house and walked to the stables once again. Entering, he stepped into the shadows, wanting to watch the activity unnoticed. Nothing stood out, however. Stalls were being mucked out, horses led out for exercise or fresh air. Water was being hauled in buckets. John walked outside again and stepped into an area which formed a walkway between the small paddocks. Pirate was there and came toward John, reaching his head over the fence to nuzzle him.

"You miss her already, don't you, old boy?" As if he understood, the horse whinnied softly. "As soon as her Bath chairs arrive, I promise to bring her out to see you. You both need that."

"Please do bring Miss Willa out," Ward said as he walked up to John. "Pirate knows something is wrong. He's moping."

John turned to the older man. "I believe horses are highly intelligent, so no doubt Pirate knows something has happened. Especially since he was there when it did."

Ward reached out to stroke the horse's nose and then looked John in the eye. "You asked me to let you know if I thought of anything or anyone who has acted suspicious."

John instantly became alert. "I did."

"A few weeks ago, a coupla young bucks stopped by to shop for hunters. Miss Willa had come into the stables for her daily ride shortly after they arrived. She musta caught the interest of one of them for he started makin' eyes at her and flirting like silly young bucks will. O' course, Miss Willa ignored him and mounted Pirate for a ride."

"I'm jealous, of course, but it doesn't seem too suspicious. Miss Willa is a beautiful young woman and attracts many covetous glances."

"There's more, my lord."

John waited patiently, knowing the stable master would get to his point in his own time.

"When they returned, Brooks told me that while those young bucks were out for a ride, Miss Willa caught up with them and surpassed them in a full gallop. When they all got back, the young buck told her he wanted to buy her horse. Miss Willa just laughed at him and said, 'I think not.'"

"Who is he?"

"I don't know, my lord. I'm not a young man, and all the gentlemen who visit the stables begin to blur for me, I'll admit."

John reached out and patted the man on his shoulder. "Its okay, Ward. I'll ask the viscount."

"I fear he won't know the answer. He was away from the estate that day and pro'bly never heard about it."

"Well then, I'll have to think of a way to casually bring it up to Miss Willa." He stroked Pirate's nose one more time and then nodded to Ward. "Thank you, Ward, for bringing this up to me. No detail is too small for us to ignore. I appreciate it." He started to walk away, intent on returning to the house to speak to Willa again.

"Please give my regards to Miss Willa," the stable master called after him. "My missus and I will say a prayer for her ever' night until she's back to normal again."

John expressed his thanks and walked toward the house. Instead of entering through the front door, John walked around the house and went through the servant's entrance and down the steps into the kitchen. There he found the rotund cook hovering over a tea tray. While he had never met the cook, he knew from Willa's stories of her times in the kitchen that the woman's name was Bessie. He spoke the name now.

The woman whirled around, a knife in her hand. Upon seeing him, her face broke into a smile. "Oh, my lord, you gave me such a fright. I don't expect to find quality in my kitchen."

John smiled in return, hoping to help the woman relax. "My kitchen at home is one of my favorite places. There is nowhere else on my estate I can find delectable tidbits to sneak between meals."

Bessie laughed as he had hoped she would. "Anytime you would like to sneak a tidbit from my kitchen, my lord, you just go right ahead."

"I was hoping to get a tea tray for Miss Willa and deliver it myself. Am I in time?"

"You are. I was just adding some lemon bars to it. I baked a fresh batch of her favorites today."

John appreciated knowing this. It seemed everyone cared for Willa, but none more than himself. His love for her was deep and lasting. "If it's ready, may I carry it up?"

"You may." The cook lifted the heavy silver tray and handed it to him after adding a second cup and saucer. It was then he saw a pretty orange chrysanthemum floating in a small bowl. Willa's lunch tray had a flower on it, as well. Here was yet one more sign of how much the staff at the viscount's home cared for his fiancée. He took the tray from Bessie and made his way up the back stairs. As John approached the door, he nodded to the footman who was stationed outside Willa's bedchamber door as a convenience to the maid within. "Do you know if Miss Willa is awake?" he asked the young footman.

"I'm not sure, my lord, but let me enquire." The footman tapped quietly on the door and waited but a few moments before Luvina opened it.

John greeted the maid and proffered the tea tray. "I confiscated this from Cook," he told the maid. "If Miss Willa is awake, I would like to cajole her into enjoying one of her favorite sweet treats and speak to her for a bit."

Luvina stepped aside and swung the door open wide. "She woke about five minutes ago, my lord."

John entered the room, his eyes solely on his affianced as she lay in the bed, her shiny brunette tresses framing either side of her face. He walked across the room and set the tray on a side table. "I brought tea," he said. "I am hoping you'll offer me a cup."

"You should have joined my parents for tea, John. I'm sure you would find them to be better company."

"Nonsense," he said. "While I have found I have grown quite fond of both of them, I do not love them in the way I do you. Now why don't you use those surprisingly strong arms of yours to pull yourself upright? You are not, after all, helpless," he teased her.

"I feel helpless," she replied with a pout. "You have no idea what it is like to not be able to move your lower limbs."

"No, I do not," he admitted. "However, you must learn to make the best of it, even if it is only for a time."

"You are goading me," she accused, "just as you did at luncheon."

John could not help but chuckle. "Perhaps I am just a little." Indeed, he was pleased to see she put her hands down on the mattress and struggled to pull herself upright enough so she could relax against the pillows Luvina fluffed behind her back. John, meanwhile, poured the tea and put one of the delectable lemon bars on the plate before handing it to her and draping a napkin across her lap. He then poured his own tea and sat on the chair next to the bed.

"Did you have a good rest?"

Willa shrugged and said, "I did sleep. The pain in my back has subsided a bit."

"Wonderful! That is good news, indeed."

He was pleased to see Willa pick up her lemon bar and take a small bite. "Cook made those especially for you today," he pointed out. "Oh, and Ward says to tell you he and his wife are praying for you."

"You were out at the stables?"

"Yes, twice today as a matter of fact."

"Did you see Pirate?"

"Yes, he is missing you."

"I've been thinking about him," she said quietly. "I remember some of what happened, and he jumped far to the side. I am thankful he didn't injure himself."

"We are lucky he did not," John assured her. "Both Brooks and Ward have been over him and over him and have found no injury."

"Will you ride him for me, John?" she asked as she turned her expressive brown eyes toward him. "He will not be happy if he doesn't get his run in."

"If you would like me to, I will." He sipped his tea and thoughtfully chewed a bite of the bar, relishing the buttery citrus flavors against his tongue. "Ward was telling me a young gentleman offered to buy him from you a few weeks back."

Willa scowled. "The jackanapes. I can't believe he was so audacious."

"Who is this audacious gentleman?"

"Mr. Alistair Penworthy, youngest son of Squire Penworthy," she answered him. "The truth is he could not afford a horse as fine as Pirate. Furthermore, he wouldn't know how to treat him and could not even stay on him; Pirate is so spirited."

John appreciated how the conversation had put some spirit in Willa's voice. He hated seeing her giving up as he had so far during the day. It was understandable, but most unlike her normal animated personality.

"He must have been angry you would not take him up on his offer."

"More irked, I believe. I doubt if he ever thought I would take him up on it. He left in good spirits, having been allowed to ride an animal far finer than any he has probably ever ridden, even if it wasn't Pirate."

The bedchamber door opened without warning, and the viscountess hurried in. "Oh, you are having tea!"

John rose politely. "Please join us, Blythe. While we may not have a lot of tea left, we can ring for more, and we do have a lemon bar to spare."

"That is quite all right," Willa's mother said as she hurried to her daughter's side and fussed lovingly with the covers, her napkin, and her hair. "I just wanted to stop in and tell you we have asked Fayre to come stay with us for a while. Abbott has already sent a carriage for her, along with one of the parlour maids. The driver is carrying a written request and will wait for her to pack before he comes back."

Willa seemed pleased with the news. "So she might be here three days hence?"

"I would think so," her mother assured her before bending to kiss the top of her daughter's head. "I love you, dear." With the proclamation she turned toward the door, Luvina in her wake.

While the maid's back was turned, John leaned forward and tucked one finger under her chin before kissing her on the lips. "And I love you, too, sweetheart."

Chapter Five

The next day Dr. Saunders declared they needed to move Willa quite often. To prevent open bed sores, the maids were instructed to roll her over onto one side or the other at intermittent times of the day or night. Pillows could be used to prop her legs in the position. Footmen were instructed to lift her with care from the bed and into a comfortable chair with arms so she might spend part of the day sitting. John requested a pair of matching arm chairs be moved next to the window overlooking the gardens at the back of the house. There, the two of them could sit and talk.

Willa had appreciated the change of scene, however, she still worried over her condition. The pain in her back was constant, although manageable without laudanum or even willow bark tea. She still had no sensation in her lower limbs and could not move them no matter how hard she concentrated. To know she might never walk or ride a horse again was a depressing thought to her. Added to this was the worry she could not be a proper wife to John and might never be able to experience motherhood.

She wasn't normally a young woman who cried much, but lately she found herself weeping most of the time. In truth, she wanted to just curl into a ball and give up. Ironically, she couldn't do it without help as she couldn't curl her legs up anymore.

John seemed determined to force her to come to terms with her condition. While he told her he loved her and she knew he did, he pushed her to help herself by using her arms and upper body to drag herself up in bed to a sitting position. He read to her, talked to her, and played games with her. She found this both infuriating and stimulating. While she wanted to hide, he refused to let her.

Five days after the accident, he was playing chess with her. He was a challenging opponent and forced her to contemplate each move. She was doing just that when the door to the bed chamber flew open and her pretty blonde cousin, Fayre popped into the room still in her traveling cloak.

"I couldn't wait to see you, Willa," the pretty blonde burst out, her blue eyes sparkling as she smiled. "The carriage trip seemed interminable when all I wanted to do was be here with you."

Willa watched with amusement as did John, judging by the grin on his face. Fayre threw her cloak off, almost hitting the maid in the face as the servant caught it. She rushed to Willa, wrapped her arms around her and gave her a squeeze. Then, as if in afterthought, she looked at John.

"Hello Lord Roydon," she said and managed a curtsy.

John laughed. "I think you should call me John, and if you don't mind, I'll call you Fayre. We're almost family after all."

"Please do call me Fayre," she replied

"How was your trip?" Willa asked.

"Other than being tiresomely long, it was fun. I do enjoy seeing the landscape roll past the window. Sarah, the maid your mother sent along, is nice, too."

"I'm glad you came. I need your sweet personality as a distraction." Then, much to Willa's dismay, tears started to roll down her face. She fumbled on her lap for the handkerchief she kept nearby and blotted at them as Fayre squatted down and wrapped her arm around her shoulders. John leaned forward and ensconced her hand in his much larger one, murmuring soothing words.

Willa struggled to bring her emotions under control and then tried to bravely smile at the two of them. "I'm sorry," she said, "I can't seem to help myself."

"It's all right," John told her with an understanding note to his voice. "It's to be expected, but now with Fayre here I think you'll be feeling much better. In fact, I'll set the chess board aside and let you two ladies have a nice visit. I'm going to go exercise Pirate." He bent and kissed her cheek in front of Fayre, then winked at the younger girl and left.

Fayre sat in the empty seat. "Have you had tea yet?" she asked.

"No," Willa replied, "but we can request it." She looked at Luvina who was on duty with her at the time.

"Of course, Miss," the maid replied before going to the bell pull.

"Now tell me," her cousin said, "are you in unbearable pain?"

"No, that is what is odd. My back hurts a small amount, but mostly it is just that I cannot move my legs or feet at all. They feel like they are just dangling there."

"Hmmm," Fayre sounded thoughtfully.

Willa continued. "When the doctor runs a sharp instrument down the bottom of my right foot, I can feel it a bit, but not when he does so on the left." She was silent for a moment before she continued. "I'm so scared, Fayre. What if I can never walk again? The doctor has told me I don't dare risk a pregnancy. I love John so much and all I want to do is marry him and have a family and now I don't know if I can."

※

John stepped out the front door and took a deep breath of the fresh autumn air. It was becoming increasingly difficult to sit in the bedchamber with Willa for hours. He was an active man and enjoyed being involved in the running of his estate, exercising his horses, and participating in a competitive hunt. Playing chess, reading books, and sitting in a chair at his fiancée's bedside was tiring for him. Moreover, watching his lovely and active bride-to-be give up and sink into the doldrums was crushing his spirit. Walking into the stables, he asked Brooks to saddle Pirate for him.

"I'm happy you're taking him out, my lord," the groom said. "He's been a bit restless today."

"I believe I'll take him down the road a bit, then," John said.

It was only a matter of minutes before he and the horse were making their way at a brisk pace in the opposite direction from the village. Pirate was enjoying a gallop when John caught a glimpse of a sign along the roadway. He pulled back on the reins and turned the horse around. Soon they were in front of a signpost at the corner of the main road and a lesser one. One of the arrows pointing south read "Townsend Park." Why did the name seem familiar, John wondered. As he took off his hat and let the breeze ruffle his hair, John remembered Ward had said Miss Marty was the daughter of the late Baron Townsend. She was the woman reputed to be good with animals. After making a quick decision, John directed Pirate onto the side road and headed toward Townsend Park.

About three miles had passed before the earl saw another sign for the estate. He steered Pirate to the west and rode onto lands which were well-kept and housed fat and sleek looking Angus doddies. The black cattle were grazing in pastures fenced with split rail fences. At the far end of the drive, he noticed a cluster of buildings, including a stately but modest home, a barn, and a number of other buildings. As he entered the drive, a footman stepped out of the house to greet him and to take the reins as John swung down out of the saddle.

"Good afternoon," he greeted the servant. "I'm looking for Miss Marty Robinson. Does she reside here?"

"Yes, sir. The butler will take your calling card to her."

As he said it, the house door swung open once again and a rotund butler appeared. John walked up the steps and proffered his card.

"Please come in, my lord," the butler said. He moved to take John's great coat, hat, and gloves. "I will alert Miss Robinson of your arrival," he continued as he walked toward a side door. It was a few moments before the man reappeared and bowed to John. "Miss Robinson will see you in the library."

John walked in, curious as to what he would see. The library was quite typical with wood paneling, two wingback chairs in front of the fireplace, and a large wooden desk facing the center of the room. The surprise came when he spied the slight figure behind the desk who looked as if she had just risen from the leather chair behind her. She could not have stood more than an inch or so over five feet and was slender to the point of appearing wraith like. Her skin was clear with a natural rosiness to her complexion, and her face was framed by a short, cropped mop of golden curls. This could not be Miss Robinson. Why, this young woman could not be as old as Willa.

"Lord Roydon," she greeted him as she made her way around the desk, revealing a trim figure dressed in a pretty pink-sprigged muslin gown with a modest neckline and long sleeves. "I don't believe we have met, although I have heard much about you." She extended her hand, and John took it in his own.

"I must confess," he stated, "I had not heard of you until recently."

"And I do hope what you have been told is of a positive nature."

"It is, I assure you," he said.

"Can you join me for tea? I asked Drake to have it served." She indicated the seating in front of the fireplace.

"Yes, tea would be nice." John seated himself in one of the two chairs as Miss Robinson sank into the opposite one. Almost immediately, the butler appeared through the open door with a tea tray filled with tempting finger sandwiches and tea biscuits.

"How do you take it?" Miss Robinson asked.

"One lump of sugar, please. I've been out riding, and I must admit this is appreciated."

"I am curious as to why you stopped in," Miss Robinson said.

"As you may know, I am to marry Miss Willa Dutton," he began "and have been staying with the family. Your name has been bandied around out in the stables, so when I saw the sign-post I decided to visit."

"Yes, I had heard you were engaged and was delighted. Miss Dutton is a wonderful young lady. She is a fearless rider and cares for her livestock well. I was upset to hear about her accident. How is she doing?"

"Dr. Saunders is unsure how she is physically," John stated truthfully. "She is suffering from paralysis from about her waist down. There is a small amount of feeling in her right foot, however, and she has some back pain where she landed on a tree root."

"That is too bad. I cannot imagine what caused her to lose her seat. It is not like her. Does the doctor have hopes she will recover?"

"Some hope, yes. I have done a bit of reading on medical topics myself and yet refuse to believe she is permanently paralyzed. I'm afraid she does, however. Her mental state is not as good as I would hope. I believe she is suffering from melancholia."

"I would be, too," his hostess replied. "It is hard to imagine what it must be like to not be able to walk or ride. If I were even housebound, I am afraid I might decide I would rather not go on living."

"Her cousin has just arrived," John said. "I am hoping she will be a bit of a distraction to Willa so she quits contemplating her future quite so much."

"Yes, that will help." Marty Robinson lifted her tea cup and sipped from it. "I am curious, Lord Roydon, about your statement of how my name has been bandied around Lord Amhearst's stables."

"To be honest, Miss Robinson, I believe someone has been sabotaging Willa's horse and tack. The only reason Pirate lost her was because her saddle girth had been cut almost clean through. When a bird hit Pirate in his belly, he leapt to the side, and there must have been just enough stress on the saddle to break the girth. Her groom said she was still sitting on the saddle when it flew off. Willa flew over the fence and landed on a tree root. I have been trying to investigate and Ward, the stable master, told me a few weeks ago Pirate had been acting skittish. He said he met you in the village and discussed the horse's behavior, and you suggested it sounded like he had gotten into some lupine."

"Yes, I do remember the conversation. I once had a horse who, I must admit, was not the most intelligent of the breed. He got into lupine and his behavior was exactly the same as it sounded like Pirate's was. I do not believe lupine would kill a horse, but it would definitely cause his behavior to be bad enough he might lose a less-experienced rider than Miss Dutton."

"I was afraid of that." John decided he would not stand on ceremony with this delightful young woman, and he reached for another tea biscuit. It had a raisin filling and he particularly loved raisins. "Do tell me, Miss Robinson, how it has come about that you are known for a distance around as to be extremely good with animals. You must admit it is most uncommon for the daughter of a peer."

She laughed. It was a rich and throaty chuckle which made John smile. "Yes, I do suppose it is most uncommon. So, Lord Roydon, is much of my behavior. I am known as an eccentric far and wide, but if you want to hear the story, you must promise to call me Marty or, if you would rather, Miss Marty like most hereabouts do."

"It is a promise, Miss Marty, and please do call me John."

"Unfortunately, while I loved my father, he was a wastrel and had not a clue about how to run a farm. My mother had already passed away before my father died when I was not yet eighteen. It took me little time to realize our staff running the farm were both untrustworthy and, I'm sorry to say, complete idiots. My young half-brother had inherited the Baronetcy and I realized there would be nothing left for his future if I did not step in. So I armed myself with books and asked questions of neighbors. I donned a pair of boy's trousers and good mucking boots, and I started working with the herd. I discovered I'm good at it – quite good. Furthermore, I love it."

John found himself grinning at her. He could not see this tiny feminine creature out mucking around in the mud, delivering calves, or facing down an angry bull. She must be one determined lady. "And did you bring the estate around?" he asked out of curiosity.

"I did," she said with pride. "My brother is still in school, but when he is finished, he will come home to an estate which is in the black. He has learned from me over school holidays, and I believe he will continue to run the farm the way I have taught him. And, if he does, he will have a solid future for himself and the family he may someday have."

John had listened to her and found he felt an enormous amount of respect for her. She was just the type of person he would want to get to know. He leaned forward, "Willa would love to ride astride and I would wager you do."

Miss Marty smiled and lifted the plate of raisin biscuits to offer him yet another. "I admit I do, however, the situation is completely different. Your fiancée has a father who is of a higher peerage than mine was. And I am firmly on the shelf with no real hopes of a quality match, so I have less reason to worry about propriety."

"Firmly on the shelf! How can you be? You appear to be no older than Willa is at a mere nineteen."

The throaty chuckle came again. "Ah, thank you for the compliment, John. However, I assure you I am eight and twenty."

John was shocked. She was near his own age. Now he was even more intrigued, but as the clock struck he realized he would soon have stayed far longer than was polite. With his stomach filled with tasty raisin tea biscuits, he set his cup and saucer back on the tea tray and prepared to take his leave.

"It has been a delight, Miss Marty, but I should return to the Amhearst's home or Ward will begin to think I have stolen Pirate."

Miss Marty rose as John did. She seemed almost surprised at herself when she said, "It has been fun, John. You should come back soon, and I'll give you a tour of the farm."

"I would like it above all things," he replied. "How about two days hence?"

"That would be perfect," Miss Marty said. "Why don't you come by mid-morning, and we'll start the tour on horseback. Then I'll have Cook fix us lunch and I will show you around the home farm afterwards."

John spoke again as he raised her hand to his lips. "I will look forward to it."

❧

Willa and Fayre were catching up over tea and crumpets. They had each received letters from Fayre's sister Claire describing her honeymoon trip. Fayre told Willa about her younger sisters and what they were doing. All the time she was visiting with Fayre, however, Willa missed John. For the past few days, he had spent much of the day with her, and now she felt somewhat abandoned. She wondered where he was and what he was doing. It was easy to understand that sitting with her had been difficult for him. John was an active man, and keeping an invalid company must be grating on his nerves.

Fayre was telling her about an incident between her youngest sister and a neighbor boy when the viscountess opened the door. "I have wonderful news, Willa my dear!"

Both girls turned to look at her. "What is it?" Willa asked, wishing it was news she would soon walk again.

"Your Bath chairs have arrived. Your father is getting a group of the servants to build a ramp out both the front door and the door into the back garden. By tomorrow at this time you should be able to enjoy the outdoors again."

Fayre clapped her hands together. "That is exciting, isn't it Willa? I declare, we will be able to enjoy many sunny afternoons in the garden now."

A footman pushed open a door and pulled a rather clumsy wheeled chair into the room. It was long and had two wheels in the back, with a third in the front. An iron handle was attached to the front wheel and Willa realized it could be used to pull the chair, or by the rider to steer it. The seating area was made of wicker and had a hood, reminding Willa of a giant child's pram. "Would you like to try it out, Miss?"

Willa didn't think the awkward vehicle was going to improve her life much, but she agreed to try. "Why not?" she asked with a shrug.

The footman wheeled the chair quite close and then moved the handle out of the way. With that, he slipped one arm beneath her useless dressing-gown-clad knees and one arm around her lower back, lifting her gently from her chair and setting her just as gently in the new monstrosity.

Willa used her arms to scoot a bit higher up into the chair just as the footman moved the handle into a more upright position and then stepped to the back of the chair. Soon, Willa was moving forward, and she realized she could move the handle to steer the front wheel much like she used the reins to direct a horse to turn. Suddenly finding herself more in the mood to use the chair, she steered the chair toward the bed chamber door. She had not been out of her room since she had awoken unable to move her legs.

Fayre and Lady Amhearst moved along behind them as they ventured down the hall toward the stairs. As they came to the head of the stairway, the front door swung open, and John strode in. He came to a halt and looked up at her.

"Willa! You are mobile again." He bounded up the stairs and walked slowly around the chair, pushing and pulling it a bit.

Looking up at the viscountess he asked, "Is there one downstairs as well?"

"There is. I had it placed in the drawing room."

"Well, this explains the pounding and sawing on the front step," he said. "As soon as they have finished the ramp, Willa, you and I are going to the stables to visit Pirate."

Chapter Six

Willa lay awake much of the night worrying about her relationship with John. She loved him so much she ached and wanted nothing more than to marry him and provide him with children. They had talked about how they would enjoy teaching their children to ride and how they would gallop over the pastures as a family. The outdoors would be where they spent much of their time – hunting, walking, and overseeing the earl's estate. And now she was crippled.

She also knew her melancholia had disturbed John. It was obvious even to her, how much he tried to lift her spirits, to get her to be more independent. Everyone talked about hope and about how the tiny bit of feeling in her right foot meant there was a chance she would walk again. Willa didn't believe it. In fact, she was confident she would be paralyzed for the rest of her life.

As she lay there in the darkness with Fayre breathing evenly in the small bed they had moved into the room upon her insistence so Molly could have a good night's sleep, Willa decided it was time she got on with her life. If she was to be paralyzed for her entire life, she needed to learn how to adapt.

Consequently, upon Molly bringing in a tea tray for the two young women, Willa told her she would dress for the day. "Pick out something cheerful for me, will you Molly?"

After Fayre had risen and both girls had enjoyed their morning tea, Molly and Fayre worked together to aid Willa in dressing. Molly selected a light woolen dress in a green the color of the moss in the forest. It had a higher neck than was strictly fashionable and long fitted sleeves which buttoned up to the elbow. The dress was a good color to bring out Willa's complexion. When paired with a lightweight shawl in a deep orange embroidered with leaves the same moss color, it was particularly complimentary. This alone gave Willa a slight boost from her melancholy.

As soon as she was dressed, Willa asked Molly to ring for a footman. She requested she be lifted into her upstairs Bath chair, wheeled to the stairway, and then carried downstairs to the Bath chair there. By mid-morning, she was settled into the drawing room with her cousin where they could look out the front windows at the men building her ramp. Much to her delight, Willa spied her fiancé there with the servants. He was in his shirt sleeves, pushing a saw through planks of wood. As though he sensed her gaze, he looked up at her. He smiled and lifted his hand in greeting before returning to his task.

Fayre and Willa watched as the last board was nailed into place. John reached for his coat and shrugged into it before striding through the front door. He popped his head into the drawing room door.

"You look beautiful today, Willa." She enjoyed the warmth of his gaze on her. As if he suddenly realized she was not alone, he turned his head and smiled at Fayre. "And look at you, Miss Fayre, so pretty in pink."

Both young women blushed and John watched their reactions before saying, "I'm just going to go clean up a bit. Then I'll be down to join you ladies and the viscount and viscountess for luncheon."

Willa sighed. He deserved so much more than a paralyzed wife.

John reappeared not more than a quarter hour later and suggested he could wheel Willa into lunch and escort Fayre on his arm at the same time. The threesome made their way into the dining room just as the viscount and viscountess appeared from separate directions. A chair had been moved away from one side of the table, and John wheeled Willa into the space. However, it quickly became obvious it wasn't going to be suitable for being close enough to the table. Instead, he backed the wheeled chair out and looked at the viscount. "I think we need the chair back, Yale." The viscount had not had time to move before a footman hurried to slide the chair back up towards the table. John then scooped Willa up and placed her on the dining chair.

Luncheon consisted of a chicken fricassee, cauliflower grown in the greenhouse, a loaf of fresh bread, and a sweet trifle for dessert. The family seemed to be excited Willa had joined them.

"How do you like the Bath chairs, Willa?" her father asked.

"It's nice to be able to escape from my bed chamber," she replied.

"This afternoon we are going to visit Pirate in the stables as I promised," John assured her.

True to his word, as soon as the meal was over, John placed Willa gently back into her wheeled chair and then made sure her shawl was wrapped securely around her. Without inviting anyone to go with them, he steered her out the front door and down the ramp. He set a brisk pace on their walk to the stables, causing Willa to laugh.

"You're laughing," John pointed out.

"Oh, I am, aren't I?" She laughed a bit more.

"It's a beautiful sound. I was beginning to fear I would never hear it again."

"I have been rather melancholy, haven't I?"

"It's understandable," he told her in a forgiving voice. "I'm sure if the same thing happened to me, I would be devastated."

He stopped to open the gate into the stable yards. "I'm glad to see you are back to more of your usual self. I missed you." A loud whinny came from within the stable. John burst out laughing. "Pirate missed you as well."

Willa had snuck both a sugar cube and an apple from the lunch table into her lap. Now, as her beloved horse put his head over the stall gate, tossed it up and down, and greeted her enthusiastically, she could not help the tears of joy streaming down her face.

"Pirate," she cried as she greeted him. The chair John maneuvered parallel to the gate caused her to sit high enough she could stroke the velvety soft nose. She giggled when the horse reached over to nuzzle her cheek. As she held up the sugar cube, she relished in the feel of his soft lips nibbling at the cube. When the horse finished, he tried to reach for the apple in her lap. "You greedy beast," she laughingly reprimanded him. "I have to find a way to cut it up first."

John held out his pocket knife, the blade carefully pointing away from her. "He wants you to hurry," he said as the horse reached farther to push at her hands and try to steal the whole apple. "It is obvious Pirate has little to no patience."

Willa took the knife and sliced the apple into quarters which she proceeded to feed one at a time to her horse. "Have you ridden him?" she asked John.

"Just yesterday, as a matter of fact. We took an energetic gallop down the road to. . ." he trailed off. "Just down the road a short distance," he finished.

❧

As soon as he said it, John wondered why he hadn't mentioned his trip to Townsend Park and how he had met Miss Marty. Somehow it hadn't felt right, and so he had changed his mind about what he was going to say. It did give him great pleasure to watch Willa and Pirate interact. While they stood there, some of the grooms and the tack boys, along with Ward, came by to greet Willa. Each of them told her they had been thinking about her and hoping for a complete recovery. As he turned Willa's chair and pushed her back toward the house, John thought perhaps he should make note of who hadn't stopped to talk to her.

"Do you want to go inside or would you rather stay out for a while longer?" he asked his fiancée.

"Definitely outside," came her reply. Then she twisted her head and looked back at him. She had not worn a bonnet and the sun glinted off her rich brown hair. It was arranged casually, loose around her shoulders, tempting a man to run his fingers through it. "Let us go to the West garden," she suggested.

"That is a good idea," John replied knowing it would be protected from the slight breeze while catching the strong afternoon sun. As he wheeled her there, he thought about what to say, how much he should tell Willa about the suspected attempt on her life. He did not want to upset her with the suspicions that someone might have wanted to injure her. Instead, he wanted to protect her from the information.

Settled in a sheltered, sunny area surrounded by brightly colored autumn flowers, John sat on a wrought iron bench next to the chair Willa occupied. He reached over with his hand and entwined his fingers with hers.

"It seemed everyone in the stables wanted to wish you well," he started.

"Yes, well at least my favorites."

"Who are?"

She looked at him. "Brooks, of course. I understand after the accident he rushed for help."

"Yes, he did. I don't believe his horse could have run any faster, and Brooks was yelling for help long before he reached the house. He had laid his jacket over you to keep you warm and was concerned about you. Who else are your favorites?"

"Jem is rather adorable, don't you think?"

"What is he, about fourteen?"

"Yes, he turned that this past summer. His father left his mother and Jem is working to help support his younger siblings.

They live in the village so he can go home each night and he has Sundays off to go to church with his family. I worry he should be going to school, but I guess it is not possible."

"How long has he worked here?"

"A little over a year." Willa was quiet for a few moments, tipping her head back to take advantage of the sun. "He does read. I asked him once and he told me his mother makes him read aloud to the younger ones each evening so she can be sure he is literate."

"He also cares about you a lot. I saw him almost in tears the day after the accident," John told her.

"I do like Ward, too," Willa told him. "I like all of them except. . ."

John encouraged her to go on. "Except?"

"Well, Jenkins is just so new I haven't had a chance to get to know him."

"When did he start?"

"Hmm," she thought before answering, "about three months ago perhaps."

"And you don't care for him?"

"It's not that, John. I just don't know him well, and I've picked up a bit of an attitude from him."

"What type of attitude?" John probed.

"I feel like he doesn't think a woman belongs in the stables, or he thinks I shouldn't enjoy riding so much. There's just something there," she trailed off.

"Perhaps he used to work for someone where the women only rode on horses that plodded along through the park," John suggested.

"It's possible," she said before changing the subject. "Where did you and Pirate ride yesterday afternoon?"

John shifted uncomfortably on the bench, hesitant again to tell her the truth. "West down the road. I wanted a good run and it didn't seem like the best choice to go toward the village."

"No, I don't suppose it would be."

Willa had noticed John seemed uncomfortable when she asked about where he had ridden Pirate. She wondered why. What harm was there in her knowing? Trying to shrug it off, she made up her mind to enjoy the rest of their excursion. The accident had kept her restricted to her room, causing her world to become quite small. Even the once small act of getting outside had improved her mindset immensely.

The two of them had sat in the garden for a bit longer, enjoying the fall weather and watching the birds flit from branch to branch. Two squirrels, their red coats getting thicker as winter approached, emerged to play in the yellowing grass. Both Willa and John laughed as they watched the creatures' antics. Going up and down the trees, hiding under bushes, twitching their plush tails playfully to attract their mates.

All too soon, Fayre located them. "Aunt Blythe sent me to fetch the two of you and warn you it was nearing dinner time," she said.

John rose and stepped behind the chair. "I suppose we should go in," he said with a regretful tone to his voice.

"Yes," Willa replied. "Perhaps we could do this again tomorrow?"

John was quiet and didn't reply until prompted with "Could we?"

"I'm afraid I have an appointment for much of the day tomorrow," he replied at last.

"Do you?" Willa wondered what type of appointment John could have in their neighborhood. "You aren't leaving are you?"

"Just for a few hours."

"It must not be too far away then."

"No," he replied, still not offering any more information.

He grew quiet as he walked them around the house and pushed her up the ramp. Fayre filled the silence.

"If John is busy, I will be happy to take you for a walk outside," she said. "If the chair is too difficult for me to push over the uneven ground, we will have a footman accompany us. I'm sure Abbott would spare one for us."

"Yes, I'm sure he will," Willa agreed.

Finally John spoke again. "I do wish you would stay out of the stables unless I or your father is with you."

"Why?" Willa was curious. She had always had free run of the estate.

"I am requesting it, that is all," he said.

"Fayre and I will enjoy the East garden in the morning, and the West in the afternoon, then," Willa assured him, again wondering about his odd behavior.

"That is a good idea," he replied. "After so many days indoors, it will be nice for you to enjoy the weather while it holds."

Seated at the dining table as the footmen served them, Willa looked up as her mother spoke. "I have an announcement," the viscountess declared. When she had everyone's attention she spoke again. "We have hired a nurse for you, Willa. Poor Molly and Luvina have been stretched to the limit, and now they will both be able to return to their own duties."

"And what will the nurse do?" Willa asked, not liking the sound of needing a nurse.

"She will help with your bathing and personal care, be available to help you stay mobile in your new Bath chairs, and make sure you are in good health."

Willa didn't reply. She did not want to be dependent on anyone, but realized she was. It was Fayre who asked the nurse's name.

"Her name is Nancy," the viscountess replied.

"When does she start?" her husband asked her.

"That is the wonderful part. She is starting at once. It is a stroke of luck she walked into the employment agency just yesterday and came for an interview on the mail coach today."

"Does she have prior nursing experience?" John asked.

"She does. She has several years of experience and excellent references." Lady Amhearst continued. "I interviewed her myself and she gave all the correct answers. I am confident she is an excellent choice and had Mrs. Bailey show her to her room immediately. Except for her night off, she will sleep in Willa's dressing room on a cot so Fayre can move into her own room next door to Willa. If Willa has a bell within reach, she will be able to call the nurse whenever she needs to. I suggested Nancy settle in a bit and this evening, Molly will introduce her to you, Willa."

"I'm not sure I need a nurse," she replied to her mother meekly.

"I do realize you would rather not, but think of it as an assistant for Molly. Why the poor girl has been spending every waking minute seeing to your needs and spending far too little time sleeping. I do swear she has dark circles under her eyes."

Willa thought about it and decided her mother was correct. As much as she hated to admit it, even with Fayre there, Molly was working far too hard. And Fayre couldn't stay forever. Why, next spring the Duke and Duchess of Lamberton would sponsor Fayre's own come out. "You are right, Mother," Willa admitted.

※

After an evening of listening to Fayre play the pianoforte while the rest of them played whist, John carried Willa upstairs to her room where he sat her on the bed with Fayre in tow. Molly brought in the new nurse and introduced her to John, Willa, and Fayre. There was something about her eyes he could not warm up to, but John tried to brush it aside and bade his fiancée and her cousin a good night before retiring to his own room.

Martin was preparing for the night as well as the next day when John entered his bed chamber. The fire had heated the room to a perfect temperature and a small tumbler of cognac sat on the table next to a comfortable chair. His dressing gown was draped across the bottom of the bed on which the covers had been pulled down.

"Good evening, my lord," the valet greeted him cheerfully. "I hope you have had a most pleasant evening."

"Thank you, Martin. I finally trounced the viscount in whist. The man is a good player and I believe he thoroughly enjoys beating me. In fact, the last time we played, he laid down the winning hand and said, 'Take that, you young pup.'"

Martin chuckled. "It does sound as if he enjoys winning." He walked over and assisted John out of his jacket. "Do you know what I should prepare for tomorrow?"

"Yes, riding clothes. I am to visit a neighboring farm and look over the livestock and the establishment, so I will want to wear my best riding boots. Perhaps the brown corduroy jacket?"

"An excellent choice," Martin agreed. As he walked away, John spoke to him.

"Have you met the new nurse, Martin?"

The valet stopped and turned around. "Yes, she dined in the servant's hall with us."

"What did you think of her?"

"I barely had a chance to meet her, my lord. Her name is Nancy, but she sat at the other end of the table from me."

"I met her tonight when I carried Willa upstairs to her room. There was something about her eyes I could not like. They seemed shifty."

"I did not have a chance to notice."

"Do me a favor, will you, Martin?"

"Anything, my lord."

"Keep your eyes and ears open and report anything suspicious to me, I have to get to the bottom of what is going on and who might be trying to harm my fiancée. And why – I must know why."

Martin smiled. "I will, my lord. In fact, tomorrow I will make it a point to get to know her, and I'll be discreet about it."

Chapter Seven

Matilda Robinson, better known as Miss Marty in the neighborhood, was looking forward to the day. John Herne, the Earl of Roydon, had a reputation far and wide as being an astute estate proprietor and a compassionate animal owner. Marty was proud of the herd of Angus doddies, and she did not get to show them off as much as she wished. A man like the earl visiting was something to be excited about, indeed.

Marty had dressed in trousers for the day and hoped it wouldn't shock him too much. When she had mentioned it, he hadn't seemed to be outraged, and it was difficult to traipse all over the pastures and throughout the barns in a gown. Furthermore, Marty had long since passed the point of caring what others thought about how she dressed. She was known as an eccentric, but it was not something which bothered her.

Marty had arranged for her cook to prepare a hearty luncheon for the two of them. Menus were not something she cared about, so she left the choice of what to serve up to her competent housekeeper and cook. Her farm manager had been warned to make sure the farm looked its best. The thought of a broken fence or a shoddy stall door made her shudder.

The butler approached as she sat in the library awaiting the earl's arrival with anticipation. Drake cleared his throat, "The Earl of Roydon has arrived, Miss." Marty rose and smiled at the aging man. "Thank you, Drake." She led the way through the library door and into the hall where the earl waited. Remembering his request to use his Christian name, she greeted him with an extended hand and a warm "Hello, John!"

John took her hand in his, "Miss Marty, what a delight it is to see you again."

Marty became aware of Drake standing behind her, holding the short-waisted coat she often wore outside. She slipped into it with his help and then buttoned the coat. "I do hope I have not shocked you too much by wearing my trousers," she spoke to John.

Marty watched as his eyes glanced over her slender body. "Not at all," he said. "I must admit I would not want to work an estate in a gown. I cannot expect you to."

Marty took her bonnet from the butler and set it atop her head, tying the bow beneath her chin. It was a bit silly with the trousers, she knew, but it was a feminine version of a top hat and less silly than many bonnets would be. She had not slipped so far into eccentricity she did not still care for her skin. Drake opened the heavy front door for them as she moved toward it.

"Shall we start out on horseback?" she asked the earl.

"That would be nice," he agreed. "One of your grooms took my horse to the stables and told me he would water the horse before we venture back out."

"This way, then." Marty indicated the stables, which were the closest outbuilding to the house.

"Will you ride astride?" John asked her, a curious but non-judgmental tone to his voice.

"Yes, I prefer to," Marty admitted, "but will also ride side-saddle when others would be put off by my riding like a man."

"Well, I won't be," he stated.

"How is your fiancée?"

"She is a little better. Not physically, there has been no change. However, two Bath chairs were delivered yesterday, so she has been able to escape the bedchamber. We visited the stables to see her horse and then spent time outside in one of the gardens. It gave her a mental boost which was sorely needed."

"Yes, it should have. I would need to be out and about even if I could no longer walk." Marty led the way into the stables where John's horse waited beside her own. A groom stepped forward and cupped his hands to give her a boost into the saddle. John mounted, and they rode out of the building and back into the autumn sun.

As they toured the farm Marty pointed out various pastures, talked about the cows, and described the watering system.

"I have heard Angus doddies can have a bit of a temper," John remarked.

Marty laughed. "Oh, at times, they can have quite a temper!" She rode on a bit and then continued, "They are the best mothers, though. The cows look after the calves far better than many other breeds. They also give an exceptionally rich milk even though they are not a milking breed."

"I have heard that," John said. "And by looking at your last spring's crop of calves I would say it is true. They are sleek and healthy and good sized animals. It appears you are indeed an expert in animal husbandry, Miss Marty."

Marty was filled with pride. "Thank you, John. It means a lot to me coming from someone with your reputation."

When they finished touring the pastures, they rode back to the stable and dismounted. "Cook should have luncheon ready for us," she told John. "I'm afraid we don't stand on ceremony much here, so it will be quite casual."

"I admit to being hungry," he replied. "I should wash up a bit first though."

"I always wash up right here in the stables," she told him, leading him to a shelf along the wall where a washbasin and a hand pump waited for use.

John insisted she wash first, and then he washed afterward, brushing her hand as he reached for the towel.

"Shall we go to the house?" Marty asked with a smile. As she led the way, she allowed herself a few minutes to contemplate how wonderful it was to have a new friend, and especially a peer. So often, those she had anything in common with were males, but of lower social standing, who were often put off by a woman who ran a farm.

As they arrived at the house, the butler swung the door open as though he were watching for them. Drake took Marty's coat and bonnet, and then went to help John. "Luncheon will be served whenever you are ready, Miss."

In the dining room, once they were seated, Marty nodded to the waiting footman who served glasses of ale and a hearty beef stew with warm loaves of bread. "This is the type of meal I enjoy the most," John told her. The footman's continuous presence lent an air of respectability to the intimacy of their dining alone.

Marty was hungry and ate with gusto, not worrying about what her new friend might think of her appetite. She worked hard and had no difficulty keeping her figure. "Cook has a treat for us to finish off our meal," she announced. "She told me she was planning on baking a fresh apple pie."

John raised his head and grinned. "Wonderful! I do hope you will give her my compliments."

"Of course," Marty said. "I often pass on my own compliments to her."

The meal passed with genial conversation about the challenges and rewards of farming. Even the butler was seen with a slight smile gracing his lips as the two laughed over the apple pie.

After the meal, they toured the outbuildings on foot. John admired the birthing barn, even though it was not in use at this time of year. He inspected the half dozen bulls which were kept in a fenced area near the barns. As they stepped out of the last barn, John took her gloved hand in his, squeezing it gently. "Miss Marty, today has been an exceptional one. I cannot express how much I have enjoyed it. And while it is time for me to take my leave, I promise you will see me again soon."

❦

The day had been dull. Willa had listened to Fayre practice the pianoforte. She had started a new stitching project, something she wasn't fond of doing even though she knew her life might now be reduced to it. The viscountess had gone to the village and come back with a stack of books which the vicar's wife was willing to loan to Willa. Willa selected one of them and had managed to read one chapter before slamming it shut and choosing, instead, to stare out the window of the morning parlour.

"I wonder where John went today," she commented aloud.

The young maid who was busy with the morning tea hesitated in her work. Fayre said, "I don't know."

Willa contemplated the maid. "You know, don't you, Penny?"

"His valet said he had ridden over to tour Townsend Farms," came the answer.

Townsend Farms. Miss Marty ran her brother's farm and John had gone to spend the day with her. Willa wasn't sure what to think. Townsend Farms was a well run local estate which John would be interested in touring. On the other hand, Miss Marty was an attractive woman who was close in age to John, single, and who shared many interests with Willa's fiancé.

Upon hearing how John had visited Miss Marty, Willa found herself in an even worse mood for the day. Over and over, she kept thinking about how much the two had in common. How pretty Miss Marty was, how intelligent, how good with animals. Combined with that were thoughts about herself. She was paralyzed and trapped in her Bath chair, having to be lifted and carried from one place to another. The doctor's words of how she not dare risk getting with child rang loudly in her memory. Knowing she could no longer share John's love of riding did not sit well with her at all.

John no doubt felt trapped, Willa decided by mid-afternoon. Engaged to a paralyzed woman, he couldn't easily end their engagement without being ruined socially. She could, however. Willa could release the earl from their agreement. The question arose in her mind as to whether she loved him enough to do what was best for him.

Fayre noticed her mood and tried to be as jovial as possible, attempting to lift her cousin's spirits. But nothing the younger girl did could nudge Willa out of her thoughts. By teatime, she was still in a quandary. She did love John, but was she unselfish enough to release him from their engagement? Furthermore, if she did so, it would require giving him a shove. Yes, she would have to force him to see how this would be better for him, because Willa was confident he would state he was happy in their relationship now. John and Miss Marty would be perfect together. They could ride neck-or-nothing through pastures filled with fat cows. Together they could have numerous babies, raising them on John's estate to be happy and healthy. Deciding she needed to see them together, Willa began to plot.

And so at teatime, when her mother commented on how quiet she was, Willa replied. "I'm sorry, Mother, but spending time in this chair makes for a dull day. I was thinking perhaps we could have a small dinner party. The neighborhood has no doubt heard about my accident and even my condition. Why not introduce them to it firsthand? Besides, while I love all of you, I would enjoy seeing someone from outside our estate."

"What a wonderful idea," the viscountess replied. "In fact, perhaps you would like to take on the planning. Fayre can assist you."

"Do you mean we would draw up the guest list, send out the invitations, and work with the staff to plan the menu and make sure all goes off well?" Willa queried.

"That's correct. It will give you the experience needed for when you have your own home to run."

Willa didn't think she would ever run her own home. However, she would need the experience to aid her mother as the other woman aged.

"I would like it. You will help me won't you, Fayre?"

The younger girl was practically bouncing in her chair with enthusiasm. "You know I will."

❦

John found himself in a good mood riding back to the Amhearst's estate. He had recognized a burgeoning respect for Miss Marty as he rode around her estate, admiring her land management and animal husbandry skills. Plus, carrying on a conversation with her over a hearty and delicious luncheon had made the meal unusually good. Now his thoughts swung to Willa. He felt bad leaving her behind today, but the truth was traveling with her would be difficult. If she had any hopes of recovery, jostling her spine in a carriage or buggy would not do it any good. Glad she had her younger cousin there to keep her company, John hoped she had had a good day.

Once he had handed his horse over to one of the grooms, he strode to the house where the butler admitted him. It was nearing dinner time, so John went to his room to clean up and change. Martin was waiting for him.

"I hope you had a good day, my lord," his valet said.

"A wonderful day."

"I am glad. I had quite an interesting day myself," his man ventured.

John looked up sharply. "Did you have a chance to investigate a bit?"

"Yes, my lord. I made sure to sit next to the new nurse at luncheon."

"And?"

"I asked a number of conversational questions about her past, and her answers were evasive at best."

"What was the sense you got from them?" John asked.

"As you have passed on your medical articles to me to enjoy ever since I expressed an interest in them, I feel I am somewhat knowledgeable on the subject."

"Yes."

"I suspect she has never been a nurse. I have picked up enough from those articles to know I would be far more qualified to serve in a nursing capacity than she is."

"I was afraid of that," John returned. "As I stated, there is something about her eyes."

"Yes, my lord, you are correct. They are shifty and dart from left to right. She rarely looks directly at you when she is speaking."

"Let us keep an eye on her," John said. "I don't suppose we can accuse her of anything when Lady Amhearst hired her and the nurse provided references. However, I will ask if perhaps Lady Amhearst has thought about writing to check those references."

A half hour later, John was wearing casual evening wear and had made his way downstairs hoping Willa was already waiting. Indeed, she was ensconced in the Bath chair in the drawing room dressed in a pretty yellow gown with her hair in tendrils framing her face. "Good evening, Willa," he greeted her.

Willa smiled at him in return. "Did you have a good day on your adventure, John?"

"I did," he replied without offering an explanation of his absence. "I rode my horse rather than taking the buggy, and it was a delightful autumn day. Did you get outside for a while?"

"Yes, Fayre and I spent time in the garden doing some planning."

"What were you planning?"

"I am bored, and Mother has told me we can host a dinner party for a few of the neighbors."

John smiled. "What a wonderful idea," he said. "Since my stay has been unexpectedly long, perhaps I should send for a larger wardrobe so I have some better evening clothes. When will it be?"

"A week hence."

John sat on a chair near her and reached for her hand. "Tell me what you have planned."

He listened as she described the menu and entertainment. "Fayre will entertain us on the pianoforte, and I daresay several of us will be happy to sing along."

"No doubt," he agreed.

"And cards. We'll have cards and perhaps parlour games. No dancing, I'm afraid."

"I believe many people will enjoy the games more than the dancing," John assured her. "How many are you inviting?"

"Not many," Willa replied. "The Hampsteads will be invited. They have a son who is not much older than Fayre. Then we'll invite the vicar and his wife, old Mr. Patton, the Sheffields. Oh, and Matilda Robinson," she added with her eyes on his face.

John almost squirmed in the chair under Willa's scrutiny. Had she learned where he had gone? He did not want her to suspect someone was trying to harm her, so explaining how he had gone to Townsend Farms to ask Miss Marty about lupine poisoning was not something he wanted to get into. After all, she had enough to worry about without being suspicious of everyone she came into contact with.

On the following day, John decided to ride into the village to post a letter to his mother. He had, of course, updated her on Willa's situation. This was yet another update, but also a plea for her to send one of the grooms to the Amhearst estate with more clothing for him. At this time he did not plan to return home in the foreseeable future. He could not do so until he knew Willa was safe.

The wind had become brisk, and Pirate, whom he was riding, was quite frisky, "feeling his oats," as the saying went. Clouds were building in the west, and John realized they were in for a storm. No doubt it would arrive much later in the day, but having no wish to get drenched, he gently touched his boot to Pirate's flank and urged the horse to an even quicker pace.

In the village he mailed his letter and then, leaving Pirate in the hands of an urchin who was dallying on the street, he stepped into one of the shops in search for a small gift for Willa – something to make her smile. He browsed for a short while until his eye was caught by a lady's fan. A smile curved his lips as he thought about a time in the park when Willa and her cousin Claire had played a rather delightful but infuriating game with their fan when they were trying to investigate the blackmail scheme Claire had fallen victim to. That fan had been ivory. This fan had ivory slats, but the fabric between was delicate, almost translucent. Woven in a deep burnished gold color, it was decorated with autumn leaves and flowers. After catching the eye of the shopkeeper, John purchased it and tucked it into the inner pocket of his greatcoat before retrieving Willa's horse and turning back toward her home.

As he walked in the house, he asked the butler where Willa was. "She is in her chamber, my lord."

John took the stairs two at a time and knocked discreetly on the door. Her maid opened the door. He could see her lying on her bed, dressed, but covered with a throw. "Is she okay?"

"I believe her back is aching, my lord." She stood back and bade him enter. He noticed the nurse hovering nearby.

As he approached her bed, Willa's eyes opened. "John," she said weakly.

"Molly said your back is aching," he said without preamble.

"It is, much worse than usual."

"Have you taken anything for the pain?"

"No, Nancy is trying to get me to take some laudanum, but you know I hate how it makes me feel."

"Yes, I realize it will make you sleep, but perhaps it would be the best thing for you."

"Maybe later." Willa reached her hand out and touched the brown wrapped parcel. "What do you have there?"

John remembered the gift he had purchased her. "A gift for you, my dear."

Willa smiled. "May I open it?"

"Of course you may." He handed it to her and watched as she untied the string from the paper.

"It's beautiful!" John enjoyed her obvious delight in the fan and told her of the memory it had brought up.

"We were so desperate at the time," Willa said. "I'm sure both you and the duke thought we were a couple of silly geese."

"We did find you a bit frustrating," he admitted. After a moment he continued. "Why don't I let you rest, and then I'll have them deliver dinner for the two of us to your room, and I'll spend the evening with you. There's a storm brewing outside, which may be why your back hurts worse than usual. Pirate sensed it coming in and was quite frisky today."

"I would like it above all things," she agreed.

"You have to promise me, though, you will let the nurse give you a small dose of laudanum to help you sleep tonight if your back still hurts at bedtime."

He waited as Willa sighed and seemed to contemplate the suggestion. "If it will please you," she finally agreed.

John kept his promise, relaxing in his own room for a time and then joining Willa for dinner. He reminded her of her agreement to take the pain killer and bade her good night somewhat early. After a drink with his future father-in-law, John retired to his own bedchamber at a reasonable hour and let Martin assist him in preparing for bed. He read for a short while before blowing out the candle and let the dashing and whistling of the wind lull him to sleep until a feminine scream of "Help! Help!" rent through the silence, jolting him awake.

Chapter Eight

John had his dressing gown pulled on and the belt tied by the time he flew out of his room. He was still shoving his feet into slippers, though, so his gait was unsteady as he focused his sights on Fayre, standing shivering in the doorway of Willa's room. Yale was pounding down the hall from the other direction, and both men reached the girl at about the same time.

"What is it?" John demanded as the young woman threw herself into her uncle's arms.

John didn't wait, but squeezed past and found his fiancée lying on the rug by her bed, while the acrid stench of smoke filled the room and charred bed covers were obvious on the lower left corner of the bed. He knelt down beside Willa and pushed her tangled hair out of her face. "Willa?"

Willa's eyes fluttered open. "John?" she croaked in a voice which came from an obviously parched throat.

Nancy emerged from the dressing room and rushed over to join them on the floor. "Miss Willa! What happened?" Her gaze rose to take in the scene before returning to her charge.

Fayre and Yale joined them on the floor, as well, while Blythe had hurried in surrounded by the butler and the housekeeper, all in their nighttime dishabille.

"Tell us what happened, Fayre," her uncle urged.

"I was having a difficult time sleeping because of the storm. The lightning and thunder were making me nervous since I'm not used to the house, so I decided to come in and see if Willa cared if I crawled into bed with her." Fayre took a deep breath and continued. "When I opened the door, there were flames all over the corner of the bed. Willa was asleep. I yelled at her, but she wouldn't wake up, so I dragged her out of the bed and laid her on the rug. Then I ran for the water pitcher and threw it across the bed. The dousing put out the flames."

John turned back to Willa and caressed her cheek. Her eyes were shut again, and she was asleep. He looked up at his future father-in-law. "Surely she could not sleep through this."

Yale said, "I wouldn't think so."

"She asked for laudanum at bed time," the nurse said.

John swore she had a defensive tone to her voice. "How much did you give her?"

The nurse's eyes shifted a bit to the left, and she looked down at her clasped hands.

"Just a few drops," came her reply.

"A few? Exactly how many?"

The young woman raised her eyes and finally focused them on John. "Six drops, my lord, just as the doctor first told Molly."

"Willa has always hated laudanum," the viscountess stated of her daughter. "She says it makes her feel drugged."

John then regarded Willa, who seemed to be resting despite the night's activity. "Yes, well, she appears to have been drugged." He paused before continuing. "We need to get Willa into a bed. It is obvious this one is not going to work."

"Excuse me," Fayre said, "why don't we put her in my room? I can sleep in the same bed with her. Willa needs someone closer by than the dressing room."

"Good idea," the viscountess chimed in. "John can you carry her?"

"Certainly," he said as he lifted her into his arms and carried her through the open door to the next room. Fayre had hurried ahead and pulled back the covers on one side of the bed. John laid Willa down and covered her up; she did not wake the entire time. Worried about her, he walked over and was so familiar as to perch on the edge of the bed. He lifted Willa's hand and rubbed it with his own. "Willa? Willa?" he hoped she would wake up.

John's hope was realized when she opened her eyes and looked around. "Where am I?"

"You're in Fayre's room," he told her. "There was an accident in your room. Do you remember anything about it?"

"An accident?" she frowned. "What type of accident?"

"A small fire. Fayre was scared of the storm and came into your room for company. She came in time to put the fire out with the water in the pitcher and basin."

"A fire?" Confusion filled Willa's voice as she swung her gaze to her cousin. "Oh, Fayre, how can I thank you?"

"Stay in my room with me," she said. "I'm always nervous in thunderstorms."

"Of course." Willa's eyelids were drooping yet again as she repeated, "A fire?"

John rose and faced Nancy, who had followed them into the other room. "Could you wake her maid and ask her to join us?"

The woman curtsied. "As you wish, my lord." The nurse hurried out of the room as though she were anxious to be away from them.

Fayre crawled onto the other half of the bed and sat up against the pillows. She fussed with the bedclothes just as the viscountess stepped in and smoothed Willa's mussed hair away from her face. John hoped the attention would drive the panicked look away from his fiancée's eyes.

As soon as Molly and the nurse returned, John asked Molly, "Did Nancy tell you about the fire?"

"Yes, she said Miss Fayre came in and found Miss Willa's bed on fire and pulled her to safety before putting out the flames."

"That's correct. Do you have any idea of what might have happened?" he asked Willa's personal maid. Although he didn't suspect her, he watched her face and eyes closely as she answered.

"No, my lord. I left Miss Willa about an hour before she planned on going to bed. She was in her night shift and was settled for the night. Miss Willa asked me to send Nancy in to her but told me I should retire and she would see me in the morning."

Lord Amhearst and Abbott stepped back into the room. Yale motioned for John to step into the hall.

"The fireplace grate was not quite put into place," he told John. "All Abbott and I can figure is, with the storm, a gust of wind blew down the chimney and swept embers out of the fireplace and across the room."

"Unless the fire was set on purpose," John said.

Yale shook his head. "I can't imagine who would want to set it."

"I'm not sure," John said, "but I will continue to try to get to the bottom of this. For now, I will not be comfortable unless their room is guarded."

Yale shifted. "You're right," he said. "If you're correct, however, we have no idea whom we can trust. Other than Abbott, you and myself, whom can we put our faith in?"

John sighed. "I know, I feel the same way. If you'll stay with them while I go to put on my clothes, I will sit up outside their room. Other than the windows, are there any other entrances and exits?"

"No," Yale replied. "And the windows do not have any ledges or even tall trees outside of them."

"Then I will take care to protect them," John said.

"Perhaps you can take a stint and I will relieve you in a few hours."

"That will work," John said.

❦

Willa awoke groggy with a bad taste in her mouth. She looked around and realized she was in Fayre's room instead of her own. Molly was moving quietly around the room hanging up freshly laundered and pressed clothes. That's when a small glimmer of memory made its way through the grogginess in her brain. Fayre pulling on her upper body as she tugged her from bed. The smell of smoke. John talking to her and telling her she was in Fayre's room.

She used her upper body to pull herself more upright in bed. "Why am I in Fayre's room?" she asked Molly.

The maid whirled around, "Oh, Miss Willa, you're awake!" She moved toward the bed. "How are you? Would you like me to fetch Nancy? She's next door."

"No," Willa replied. "You didn't answer my question, Molly."

"I'm sorry, Miss. I've been instructed to tell Lord Amhearst when you are awake. I'll let him know."

Willa watched as her maid moved to the door and spoke to someone outside it. She recognized Abbott's voice. Why was he outside her door?

Just as Molly shut the door, it reopened and Nancy hurried in.

"Are you awake now?" she asked.

"I am, but please don't give me a full dose of laudanum again, Nancy. It does make me feel drugged."

"But you were in pain."

"I would rather deal with the pain than the effects the medicine has on me," Willa stated emphatically. She then directed her attention to Molly. "I'd like to wear the dark blue sprigged muslin today, Molly. It's comfortable, and I have a lot of preparations to go over for my dinner party. I can't believe it's only a few days away!"

"Yes, Miss Willa."

There was a soft tap at the door, and it swung open to reveal her father. He walked across the room with purpose, pulled up a chair, and sat down next to her bed. Looking at Molly and Nancy, he said, "Would you mind stepping out for a few minutes?"

Both of them curtsied and left the room.

"What is it, Papa? Why is Abbott posted outside the door?"

"I'm not sure how to say this," her father said.

Willa grew both more curious and worried, "Just say it, Papa. It's the best way."

"Do you remember John telling you about how, in the night, your bed caught on fire?"

"I do, but it's all a bit blurry."

"Fayre was scared by the storm since she's not used to this big house. She came in to crawl into bed with you, and instead she found fire consuming your covers and the mattress at an alarming rate. We're lucky that she acted fast and pulled you from the bed. You didn't wake up, and she more or less had to drop your lower body to the floor beside the bed. Then she grabbed the water basin and pitcher and put out the fire before calling for help."

"How would my bed catch on fire?"

"We don't know," her father admitted. "There is a chance a gust of wind blew down the chimney and an ember from the fire flew across the room and landed on the bed covers before bursting into flames."

"That seems a little outrageous," she said suspiciously. "Was I burned?" She realized if her legs had been burned she wouldn't feel it.

"No, you're fine. Your mother checked your legs, and we decided not to call Dr. Saunders out in the night because she could see no marks on them." He paused. "Fayre saved your life."

"I wonder how I'll ever thank her," Willa mused, still troubled by the thought of a fire on her bed.

"I don't believe she feels she needs thanks."

Willa was silent and then, as she had a chance to organize her thoughts, she looked up into the dear face of her father. "Or someone set it on purpose."

"Or there is that," the viscount agreed. "On that chance, John and I split out the night guarding your door and of course, Fayre was here with you. Abbott took over about an hour ago and John is sleeping in. When he arises, we will discuss the situation."

"Why would anyone set my bed on fire?"

"We haven't told you this, Willa, but the saddle girth was cut, and John has done some investigating and found there have been other attempts to harm you. Your bridle was tampered with, but the tack boy caught it and repaired it. And do you remember when Pirate was acting a bit skittish?"

"Yes." Willa had a sinking feeling in the pit of her stomach.

"Well, Ward saw Miss Marty in town later on and she told him his behavior was typical of a horse who had been poisoned with lupine."

Willa experienced a sudden flash of anger. "They hurt my horse!" she said with vehemence. "That is not acceptable. I want to meet with you and John. It's my life."

The viscount leaned forward and kissed his only child on the temple. "I'll make sure you are told when we are ready to meet." With that, he rose and moved toward the door, turning when his hand touched the door knob. "I'll send Molly and Nancy back in. Keep your eyes open dear and remember Abbott, whom we know we can trust, is stationed outside the door."

Willa thought about the events which had happened. It was hard to imagine anyone would want to hurt her, but when faced with the evidence, it seemed likely it was the case. The idea of an ember flying across the room to light her bedding on fire was absurd. Yet, there could be a chance the fire started that way. However, there was no way the saddle girth was cut by accident.

The meeting took place behind the sturdy closed doors of the library with only four in attendance — the viscount and viscountess, the earl, and Willa. Tea had been served, and plates of delicacies rested on their laps as they held cups of tea in their hands. Lord and Lady Amhearst were comfortable in the wingback chairs near the fireplace. Willa sat in the Bath chair close to her father, while John had pulled up a desk chair between the two women.

"Let's start," the viscount spoke, "with listing the happenings which make us question this. My dear," he looked at his wife, "I believe you volunteered to be our secretary."

Blythe Dutton took one more sip of tea and set her cup on a side table. She had pencil and paper in hand. "I'm ready."

"There was the possible poisoning of Pirate," Willa said, leaning forward in her chair. "That infuriates me."

"And the tampering of the bridle which Jem caught," the viscount added.

"We cannot forget the worst of the attempts," John said, "the cutting of the girth strap."

"Do you remember when my horse dumped me in the pond?" her father asked Willa.

"Of course. You were soaking wet."

"John and I wonder if it was an attempt to harm you instead. The groom swears he saw a rock fly out from a bush as though it had been shot by a slingshot just as you urged Pirate ahead of me."

"So perhaps my competitiveness is what kept it from hitting my horse instead of yours?"

John spoke next. "It does seem suspicious, Willa."

"Shall I add it to the list?" her mother asked.

It took little thought. "Yes, Mother, I believe you should."

"The question is," Willa's father said, "who could want to harm you? I no doubt have enemies, but you?"

John appeared thoughtful, "Unless they are trying to hurt you by harming your only child."

"In any case, while we have a number of employees on the estate, a stranger who came by often would stand out."

"And a stranger wouldn't have access to Willa's bed chamber in the night. The house is locked," the viscountess stated.

"I think we have to assume it must be someone who works here," John said, "whether they instigated it or someone hired them. I believe we might have two suspects – one in the house and one in the stables."

Willa watched as her father rose and walked to his desk. He opened a drawer and soon came back with a ledger. "I have a list of all employees here," he told them. "Why don't we go over them and make a list of anyone we are sure is not suspect and anyone who might be more suspect."

"In what order do you have them written?" John inquired.

"Longest serving to newest," Yale replied. "Of course, many of them have been crossed off over the years as they have moved on, passed away, or retired from service."

"Why don't we start at the end? It seems to me your most trusted retainers are no doubt the ones who have been here the longest, while the newest would be more suspect."

Willa chimed in. "Our newest is my nurse, Nancy. Isn't it right, Papa?"

"It is," the viscount confirmed.

"I have only met her a few times, but I cannot like her," John added his opinion. "For example, last night when I was asking her about how much laudanum she had used to dose Willa, she wouldn't look me in the eye."

Willa looked at him. "I have taken note of that myself. She seems," and here Willa paused before finishing with, "shifty."

John smiled at her and reached over and squeezed her hand. "That is exactly what my valet had to say about her. I suggested he speak to her in the servants' hall during one of their meals. He told me she tended to avoid answering his questions about her past and how he felt he knew more about medicine than she did." Here, he turned back toward the viscountess. "I've wondered, Blythe, if perhaps you should write to those who provided her references."

"I will do so today," she assured them.

For the next half hour, they made a list of employees they were not secure in saying were trustworthy. The list was not long, with three working in the house and two in the stables. Plans were made to check their references which had been provided, as well as to interview the longer serving employees about these workers. At last, they decided they had done what they could. The viscount and viscountess prepared to write for references. John rose and smiled at Willa. "Why don't we find Fayre? Perhaps she would be so kind as to fetch your shawl, and the three of us could take a stroll before dark. It's a bit brisk outside, but I think you'll enjoy it."

"Yes, let's."

Fayre was amenable to a walk and more than willing to fetch Willa's shawl. John wrapped it around her himself and then guided the Bath chair out the front door and down the ramp. He held out his arm for Fayre, "Take my arm, Fayre." After she did so he continued, "I am a lucky man to be escorting two such beautiful young women on a walk."

Fayre giggled, and Willa tipped her head back to look up at him. "You could, however, be lucky enough to be escorting two women who can both walk rather than having to push one of them around in a wheeled chair," she said as she tried to force a light note into her voice.

Little did he know she had been thinking a lot lately about releasing him from their engagement. In fact, she thought she could help him find a woman who would be a far better choice for a wife than she would be.

"I do sympathize with you, Willa, but I am happy with my choice. I still hold out hope you will one day walk again."

Willa turned back to face forward. "I cannot imagine it will happen," she said. "I'm coming to terms with the fact I will always be wheeled around in this chair."

Fayre reached around with her other arm to touch her cousin's shoulder. "I, too, hold hope you will walk again, Willa. Why, the last time Dr. Saunders visited, you still had some feeling in your one foot."

"Some feeling, but no movement."

Chapter Nine

The night of her dinner party, Willa asked Molly to help her prepare with care. Willa had a number of lovely dresses from her come out which no one in the country would have seen. The one she selected for this night was light mint green with vertical rows of ribbon in darker green sewn from the bodice down the skirt. The sleeves were long and of the same darker shade with rows of tiny mint green buttons running up the outside to her elbow. A small mint green ruffle adorned the hem. With this she would carry a lightweight ivory shawl and the new fan John had given her.

Willa was both anxious and depressed. She refused to allow herself to reveal it to anyone, however. Her aim was to observe John in the company of Miss Marty. The more she thought about it, the more she was sure she should release John because of her love for him. It was not fair for him to be tied to an invalid wife at such a young age. Furthermore, the knowledge that she now had to be vigilant about someone trying to harm her or even kill her put her on edge.

As soon as Molly was done arranging her hair in a graceful chignon at the back of her head with tendrils teasing each cheek,

Willa asked to be carried to the ground floor and deposited in her Bath chair. She had arranged for one of her favorite footmen to assist her for the evening. His name was Morton. He was about her age, perhaps even younger, and struggled with maintaining the stoic face which footmen were expected to display. At times, she could see his eyes light with humor and there would be a barely noticeable quirk to his lips. This endeared him to her.

"You'll hover on the sidelines, won't you Morton? Then any time I want to be wheeled somewhere else, I'll look at you and nod."

"Yes, Miss Willa. I will do as you say. It's an honor. Abbott usually suggests I stay behind the scenes at social gatherings."

"I know he does," Willa said, "but I trust you."

John was the first to join her, dressed in fashionable trousers and a fitted jacket – both made of dark superfine. His crisp linen shirt was barely visible under the skillfully tied cravat. He raised her hand to his and kissed the back of it. "Willa, you look ravishing."

Willa couldn't help but smile. "Why, thank you, fine sir." For effect, she snapped open her new fan and moved it flirtatiously. He chuckled in response as she expected he would. They were interrupted by Fayre almost dancing into the room, delightfully dressed in pale pink trimmed with ribbons and bows as befit a young lady of her age.

"I can't wait until someone arrives," she announced. "I trust I won't embarrass you, cousin dear. I have been trying to recall Mama's lectures about manners."

"Oh, Fayre, you're delightful! You couldn't possibly embarrass me. When you play the pianoforte tonight, I'll be so proud of you."

"Yes," the viscountess agreed as she entered the room on her husband's arm. Blythe was dressed in a deep golden satin with her favorite topaz ear bobs dangling from her lobes. "Your uncle and I will both be proud of you, as well. This is a good rehearsal for when you make your own come out."

Due to the casualness of the evening, they had left the drawing room doors open so they all turned expectantly when they heard the knocker fall onto the front door. Within minutes, Abbott appeared followed by a middle-aged couple dressed in their best finery.

"Vicar and Mrs. Wright," the butler intoned in his most austere voice.

The two greeted their hosts and soon approached Willa. "We are so happy you invited us," Mrs. Wright said. "We have heard you are doing well, despite your injury."

"Yes, as well as can be expected," Willa replied. "I am thankful for this chair, for without it I would be bound to stay in one place all the time." Remembering her manners she introduced John. "I would like to make you known to my fiancé, John Herne, the Earl of Roydon."

Mrs. Wright, clearly flustered, curtsied. John reached for her husband's hand. "There is no need to stand on ceremony tonight. We are to be a casual gathering of friends and neighbors. It is my pleasure to meet you, Vicar and Mrs. Wright." Once he had shaken the man's hand and smiled at his wife, he indicated Fayre. "And this lovely young lady is Miss Willa's cousin, Miss Fayre Stuart."

"Why, you are such a beautiful young woman," Mrs. Wright said, "and, if I am correct, the sister-in-law of a duke now."

"Yes, thank you."

A clearing of a throat sounded at the door and Abbott escorted in the local solicitor and his wife, Mr. and Mrs. Hampstead. The couple was accompanied by their son, Ronald, whom Willa knew to be just one year older than Fayre. It was amusing to watch the two be introduced. Fayre smiled coquettishly at him and he blushed to the top of his ears.

Within minutes, the company had been joined by the elderly Mr. Patton. One of Willa's favorite neighbors, he had served in the early years of the Napoleonic Wars as a captain in the Royal Navy. Indeed, he had earned quite a reputation for himself and had many entertaining tales to share. Willa suspected they were often both exaggerated and glamorized, but they did make for riveting entertainment. Mr. Patton used a cane due to an old injury to one leg, and his hearing had been affected, no doubt by the exposure to cannon fire.

It wasn't long before the local baronet, Sir Sheffield, and his wife arrived accompanied by Miss Matilda Robinson. "We offered to give Miss Marty a ride in our carriage," the man said. "Her brother's estate borders ours," he explained upon meeting John.

Willa snapped to attention, covertly watching John with Miss Marty. John took her hand and she smiled up at him. "Hello, my lord, it is good to see you again."

"As it is you," he assured her.

Miss Marty then turned to Willa. "Miss Dutton, I was so sorry to hear about your accident."

"Thank you," Willa replied. "John told me how you were able to help Ward diagnose Pirate's behavior a few months ago. I do appreciate it."

"It's nothing. You know I love animals and do not wish harm to come to any of them."

Abbott's voice sounded over the conversation. "Dinner is served."

John moved to wheel Willa's chair into the dining room. Morton followed almost silently behind. In the dining room, John picked Willa up and set her in her chair next to her father. Once he had done so, he left the Bath chair to be moved by Morton and he walked around the table to sit next to the viscountess. Miss Marty was seated to his left.

The conversation flowed during the meal, shared by those who had spent a lifetime living in the close proximity of a small, rural community. Willa had been advised by her mother to keep the menu simpler than she would in town. The neighbors were not of a high rank and seldom, if ever, attended London events. Therefore, she had started the meal with chestnut soup. It was over this course when she overheard John say to her mother,

"Willa selected an excellent soup for the evening, don't you feel, Blythe?"

"Oh, yes, indeed. I happen to know it is a particular favorite of hers."

At this, Miss Marty joined in. "I'm so glad she did. I haven't had this soup in quite some time, and it is always a good choice."

When the soup was cleared and the next course served, Willa accepted a slice of beef from her father. A footman served her a helping of roasted turnips with a brown butter sauce. Willa waited patiently for a serving of turbot in lobster sauce, and some peas. As she lifted her fork, Sir Sheffield complimented her on her menu choice.

"It is my understanding you undertook the planning of this evening's party," he spoke.

"Yes, my mother suggested I do as it would give me something to fill my time. You know I cannot be as active as I am accustomed to."

"Miss Dutton, you planned an exquisite menu," he said as he scooped a bite of roast chicken into his mouth. "The earl is a lucky man to be marrying you."

"Why, thank you," Willa said weakly, thinking about how she could not even cross one ankle over the other. She looked across the table, eavesdropping the best she could over the sound of china and cutlery and enthusiastic conversation.

"One of my cows gave birth to an off season calf today," Miss Marty was telling John. "I may have to sell the bull which sired the calf. A fence means nothing to him."

"And how is the mother and calf doing?" John asked, obviously intrigued by Miss Marty's choice of dinner conversation. Willa knew it wasn't a common dinner topic, but also realized that Miss Marty no doubt cared little if others thought she was eccentric. Perhaps, she would one day have a reputation as an eccentric as she grew old alone, Willa mused.

"Oh, quite well," Miss Marty answered John's question with pride. "The calf is a strapping young fellow and his mama is proud of him to the point of being rude to us."

"Feeling a bit over protective, is she?"

"I have not sprinted so fast in quite some time. I was thankful I had on my trousers. I'm sure I would have been knocked flat had I been hampered by a skirt."

Willa talked absently with her father and Sir Sheffield, while paying no attention to what she was eating. Instead, her eyes and her thoughts were on the man across the table. While he spoke to her mother throughout the meal, his attention seemed to be riveted on Matilda Robinson. Humor often curved his lips and he laughed from time to time.

Miss Marty, too, seemed to be enjoying herself. She wasn't a coquettish female and didn't seem to be flirting, but she was conversing enthusiastically with John. Willa found her own mood changing to one of melancholy and she mentally reminded herself that, as hostess, she needed to stay happy.

Indeed, the dessert did help. Willa had talked to Cook about making her favorite sponge cake. It wasn't fancy, but it was light and airy. Served with a side of almond cream and bowls of fruit and nuts, it was the perfect ending to the meal. The company seemed to enjoy it, too. It was a cheerful group which split up at the end of the meal.

Morton lifted Willa into her Bath chair and pushed her into the drawing room. The other women followed, and they were soon settled with cups of tea, anxious to talk once again. Willa looked up in time to see Matilda Robinson walk into the room. "Miss Marty," she spoke, "please join me. I feel I have barely gotten to talk to you." She indicated the chintz chair to her right.

The other woman did so, settling into the chair and arranging the folds of her skirt. Willa admired her dress. It was burgundy, embroidered around the hem and neckline. "You look resplendent in that color, Miss Marty."

"I can say the same about you. Green compliments your complexion so well."

Willa thanked her and then approached the subject she wanted to get to. "I noted how much John enjoyed talking to you about cows this evening."

Marty laughed. "I do hope not everyone could hear us. I am well-bred enough to know livestock is not an appropriate subject for a dinner party, but I just couldn't resist. Your fiancé has a reputation as an outstanding estate owner."

"Yes, he does care about the land and his livestock."

"When he visited our farm, it was quite obvious," Marty said. "I enjoyed giving him a tour that day."

This was what Willa had wanted to know. He had visited long enough for a tour of Townsend Park Farms. She didn't have time to sink into despair, however, before the gentlemen joined them. It was the vicar who suggested Fayre entertain them on the pianoforte, and soon Willa's cousin was seated at the instrument with Ronald Hampstead standing at her side to turn the pages for her. John appeared at Willa's side and whispered in her ear, "Let's sing." Without waiting for an answer, he pushed her chair toward the instrument and raised his voice just as Willa joined in.

The music helped to chase her melancholy away, and they entertained the group for a half hour before Willa smilingly called it quits and suggested they play cards. Fayre and her companion chose to continue providing music, so they made an easy group of three tables. Willa found herself seated with John, Miss Marty, and old Mr. Patton. This gentleman told tales throughout the game until they were seldom paying attention to the cards. Despite her preoccupation with thoughts of John and Miss Marty the evening sped by, and Willa soon found herself bidding her guests good night.

As the door closed on the last guest, John lifted her hand to his lips. "You were born to be a hostess, Willa. The evening was perfect and everyone had a good time."

"I will agree," the viscount joined in.

"Willa, you did do a wonderful job of planning and carrying off the party," her mother agreed. "I admit it was relaxing for me not to have to be involved. I have never enjoyed a party we have hosted more." Blythe bent and kissed her daughter on the cheek. "I believe I'll retire for the night now."

"I'll walk up with you, Aunt Blythe," Fayre said as she bade the others good night.

Willa was tired and she turned to the two men. "Would one of you be willing to carry me upstairs so Morton and Abbott can both seek their own beds?"

"Of course," John said as he stepped forward and lifted her into his arms, carrying her up the stairs, past the upstairs Bath chair and straight into the room where both Molly and Nancy awaited with Fayre.

Since the fire, Fayre and Willa had shared Fayre's room. The bed in Willa's had been replaced and the room well aired, but for safety purposes, they had made the decision to leave the two girls together. Fayre had been asked if she would mind, as it could put her in danger as well. The younger woman had refused to be worried. Instead, she had pointed out how if they stayed together, Fayre would be able to lock the door after the maid and the nurse left for the night and, if there were a need, she could unlock it again when Willa required any assistance. The arrangement was working well.

The next day Willa was quieter than usual. Everyone remarked on it, prompting Willa to claim she was a bit tired. When John went to the stables to exercise Pirate, Willa asked Fayre to take her into the garden for a bit of morning sunshine. Fayre brought the book she was reading along and offered to read it aloud to Willa, but Willa declined. As Fayre occupied herself with the book, Willa thought about her future with John. She knew she should tell him she no longer wanted to marry him. He should look for someone else, someone like Miss Marty. Willa's heart ached every time she dwelt upon the subject. She loved him so much that the decision was an extremely difficult one to make.

The decision she did make was to try to visit Miss Marty Robinson. Willa felt she needed to speak to the other lady and get a sense of how Miss Marty felt about John. How to get there was the challenge. She didn't want anyone along except, perhaps, Fayre. If she told either of her parents or John of her plans, someone would offer to escort her. Instead, she decided she needed to just tell them she felt cooped up and needed some fresh air. Of course, a ride in the carriage offered little if any fresh air. Then she remembered the pony trap. The little trap was used by those who needed to go into the village, such as the cook or housekeeper. And so she made her decision.

She interrupted Fayre. "I think I'll ask Papa if we can take a ride in the pony trap."

Fayre stopped reading and looked up at her. "Won't it be uncomfortable for you?"

"I don't see how it could be any more uncomfortable than sitting in this chair or lying in my bed," Willa replied.

"Then that would be fun," Fayre agreed. "When?"

"I think I'll ask him at luncheon. Then, if we get the okay, we'll go tomorrow in the afternoon. I daresay the weather will be nice, and I do know how to drive a small gig. It will just be the two of us, but we can have Brooks ride along on horseback since I suspect we will not be given permission without agreeing to it."

With her decision made, Willa said to her cousin, "I'm sorry I interrupted your reading. Do go on."

"I have just a bit of this chapter left," Fayre said, "I'll finish it quickly."

When they were gathered in the dining room for their luncheon, Willa inquired about Pirate. "John, how was my horse this morning?"

"He is in fine fettle," John said. "In fact, I don't believe I've ever taken a brisker ride upon his back. He is still missing you, though, and I think we should take a trip to the stables this afternoon so you can visit him."

The thought made Willa smile. John took her out at least every other day. "Yes, let's," Willa agreed as she reached for the fruit bowl to take an apple and put in her lap for the horse. With that done, she turned toward her father. "Papa, I've been thinking how I would love to get out a bit more than I do. I have Fayre to go with me. Consequently, I was wondering if we could take the pony trap out for a drive."

The viscount regarded her. "You and Fayre want to take the pony trap out?" The tone of his voice was thoughtful, but not astounded. But then her fiancé broke in.

"I could take both of you out for a ride in a gig," he offered.

"I'm sorry, John, but the pony trap only holds two, and I have already promised Fayre."

John's lips quirked in amusement. "Your father does own other gigs, my dear."

"I am most fond of you, John," she said, "but I am feeling the need to test my independence. I thought to take Brooks along on horseback so, if for any reason, I need some assistance, he will be there. Also, I think I will ask him to strap my chair onto the back in case we get as far as the village and I want to go into one of the shops."

The viscount considered this, and then looked at John. "I don't see any harm in it with Brooks along for safety, do you, John? Willa is quite capable of driving it, and if we ask the stable to hitch old Pokey to it, I don't see how they can come to much harm."

Willa thought about Pokey. The elderly sorrel was over-weight, and his fastest speed was a slow, plodding gait. She would have liked a brisker pace but knew better than to push it, so she stayed silent.

"I do know Willa is more than capable of driving it," John agreed. "My only worry would be if they should come to any harm, but if Brooks is in attendance and is well armed, I do trust him to be concerned over her safety."

And so it was agreed that the next afternoon, Willa and Fayre could take a slow jaunt into the countryside. Little did any of the others know, Willa would be driving directly to Townsend Park Farms and would arrive just in time for tea.

Chapter Ten

Marty was dressed in trousers and her short-waisted jacket, leaning on a fence and studying her favorite bull when she heard the sound of a vehicle making its way down the road toward the buildings. Turning, she thought she recognized Willa Dutton and her younger cousin in a pony trap with a groom riding a horse behind them. As they drew closer, she became confident she was correct and, keeping Willa's condition in mind, she walked over to meet them on the road.

"Good afternoon," Marty called to the two younger women.

Willa drew the pony trap to a halt. "Good afternoon," she greeted. Her cousin almost simultaneously offered the same greeting.

"Thank you again, for the wonderful party, the night before last. I haven't been out socially in recent months and I vastly enjoyed myself."

Willa smiled. "I enjoyed myself as well, and I know Fayre had a wonderful time." Here her cousin nodded and agreed with an "I did."

Marty remembered her manners. "You caught me at work, but I was just about to go in and have some tea. I see you brought your chair along. Why don't you drive on up to the house and come in? I can change and join you."

"Fayre and I would love to join you for tea, but please don't change on our account. I am not put off in the least by your trousers."

"Neither am I," Fayre said. "In fact, I am a bit jealous of the freedom they offer you."

"Well, then," Marty replied, "Let us make our way to the house." She turned and strolled off at a brisk pace and arrived only moments after the pony trap had. A footman had come out to assist, and Marty watched as he carried in the bath chair and Willa's groom carried her inside. Soon they were settled in the front parlour while Drake went to bring in tea.

"I overheard you telling John at dinner you have a bull which jumps the fences," Willa brought up.

"I do, indeed. In fact, the fine fellow I was having a conversation with when you arrived is the scoundrel."

"Miss Marty, you said you might sell him."

Marty couldn't help but sigh. "Yes, I know people see me as odd, but I believe each animal has its own personality, and I like his. However, I have had to have the staff add to the top of the fence, and I have to keep him confined or he wanders all over the neighborhood. I do not believe he's happy having his activities restricted. It might be best for all if I find him a new home where his roaming is more acceptable. There is a farmer in the wilds of Scotland I know who has quite a bit of land, and he might appreciate a spirited yet sweet-tempered bull."

Willa seemed thoughtful for a few minutes as Drake brought in the tea and the three women busied themselves with their afternoon refreshment. Marty watched as young Fayre's eyes lit up when she bit into one of Cook's shortbread biscuits. "This is delicious," the younger woman said. "I do adore shortbread."

Willa sipped her tea and then looked up at Marty with a serious look on her face. "So you care enough about your bull to set him free?"

Marty found it to be somewhat of an odd statement but replied without hesitation. "That is correct. I like him and I want him to be happy."

❧

Willa listened to Marty's reply and took it to heart. She spoke again, changing the subject. "When will your brother be finished with his schooling?"

"This coming spring," Marty said. "It will be wonderful to have him home for good. The school holidays never seem to be long enough. Of course, then I am sure he will want to spend a bit of time in London as most young men do."

"Certainly," Willa agreed, "The season will be in full swing. In fact, the two of you could go to London."

"Oh, I won't attend the season. I have had mine – two in which I did not take –and I am perfectly happy to stay on the farm and keep my brother's inheritance profitable."

"I'm sure you have taught him much about running a farm," Willa stated.

"And it is a beautiful farm," Fayre put in. "Even though it is autumn, everything is so green and well kept."

"Thank you," Marty responded, "And yes, I have taught my brother how to be a good estate manager. In fact, someday I'll be superfluous."

Willa noted how quiet Marty became with the statement. She realized what a position the other woman was in. When her brother married and had children, Marty would become the maiden aunt. No doubt, her brother's future wife would not be as understanding about Marty's somewhat eccentric dress and expertise, either. Miss Marty would be in the way if she did not marry and move to a home of her own.

As tea came to a close, Willa and Fayre thanked their hostess. Then Brooks was called to carry Willa to the pony trap and strap the chair onto the back before the two girls tooled home and he followed close by, no doubt keeping an eye out for any perceived dangers.

❧

Back at home, Willa was greeted by John. "Did you have a nice outing?" he asked.

Willa hesitated, unsure of what to say. It was Fayre who filled the silence. "Oh, yes, it was lots of fun. We drove over to Townsend Park Farms and had tea with Miss Marty."

Willa watched as her fiancé raised his eyebrows. "So you didn't end up in the village?"

"No," Willa spoke. "We went west onto the road and when I saw the sign I thought it might be fun to visit Miss Marty since she seemed to have a good time at our dinner party. Miss Marty is a lovely woman, albeit a few years older than me." As Willa spoke, John stepped to her side and scooped her into his arms, carrying her up the front steps and into the house. "You seemed to enjoy her company," Willa continued.

"Yes, she is unusually knowledgeable about livestock," he said, gently setting her in the wheeled chair which was waiting just inside the front door. "You must admit, it is not often one meets a female who knows so much about animal husbandry. Of course, you are knowledgeable with horses."

"Oh, I don't know," Willa said, "I don't believe I am. Indeed, I am a skilled rider," she said without arrogance, "but I have never assisted in the birth of a foal or nursed a horse to health after an illness or injury. I do know good blood when I see it, but I am not nearly as knowledgeable as Miss Marty."

"I take it there were no mishaps or threats along the way."

"There were not, and Brooks was practically breathing down our neck the entire way and I swear he kept his hand on his pistol during the entire time."

"Good. I'm worried about your safety."

Willa grew quiet. "I must admit I am a bit worried myself."

❧

The next day, John had come in from exercising both Pirate and his own horse when the butler told him the viscount wanted to see him when he had a moment. John joined the older man in the library. "You wanted to see me, Yale?"

"Yes, I did. I have been thinking about sending for a physician from London – a second opinion, if you will. I know you are a well-read man, and I wanted your thoughts on the idea."

John sat down in the chair across from the viscount's desk. "I believe it is a good one. Perhaps we could not only check with some physicians, but also talk to men of science at Oxford and Cambridge. I think we should start at the Royal College of Physicians."

"Yes," the viscount agreed. "I was wondering if you would travel up to London and seek the advice of some of these men. I am willing to go myself, but you are more learned in the area of medicine. Also, I don't think we should both leave. One of us needs to be here to protect Willa."

"Definitely," John replied. "I could certainly ride up. I wouldn't take a carriage, just my horse, and I could travel light. It would be a good time for Martin to travel back to my estate again and pack a few more things for me. I don't intend to leave Willa until she is better or we get married, whichever comes first, provided you are not adverse to my continued presence."

"I enjoy having you here," the viscount replied. There was a knock at the library door, and Yale called, "Enter." Abbott opened the door, holding a box bound in brown paper and string.

"I thought you should know, my lords, this was left on the front step. I heard a knock, but when I opened the door there was no one there, just this. It is addressed to Miss Willa."

John rose from his chair and strode across the room to take the package. He frowned when he took it. It was not heavy, but the weight seemed off, as though the contents were all on one side. As he moved it, the weight moved, yet there was no sound coming from it, such as the sound of an object rolling around.

He thanked the butler and took it across to the desk where he sat it. "I have a bad feeling about this," he told the viscount. "It is as if the contents are moving around within the box, yet it makes no noise."

The viscount stood and reached across the desk to pick up the box and tilt it a bit. John watched as Yale frowned. "I see what you mean," he said. "I suggest we open this box for my daughter and, perhaps, we would be wise to step outside."

"A weapon might not be amiss," John suggested.

"Pistol or sword?" the viscount asked.

"I'm not sure. Why don't we take both, but perhaps have the sword unsheathed since it would be faster than the pistol?"

"I keep the sword above the hearth sharpened," the viscount said. "I'll load my pistol if you would be so kind as to retrieve the sword."

Both men reached for their individual weapons and Yale carried them out. John carried out the box. Outside the French doors, he set the box on the flagstone about ten feet from the house. They had shut the doors behind them and John looked at his future father-in-law. The viscount was not a corpulent man; however, he was older and had more girth than John. "Why don't you stand away and let me have the sword? I am younger and perhaps a bit quicker on my feet."

"I won't argue with you there, son." Lord Amhearst stepped about half the distance to the house.

John took the sword in his hand and reached over to insert it between the box and the string, pulling up against the taut twine. He felt a certain amount of satisfaction when the sharp blade sliced through it. Taking a deep breath, John then used the tip of the sword to slice the paper around what was obviously the lid of the box. Finally, he used the sword to flip the lid off the box. Almost immediately, a snake with an all-too-familiar distinctive dark zigzag slithered from the box and struck at John. Feeling it strike his knee-high leather boots, John brought the sword down upon the snake, quickly severing the reptile's head from its body.

"An adder," the viscount said. "Someone sent my daughter a poisonous snake. This makes it clear they are trying to kill her."

John realized his hands were shaking. He leaned over to inspect the dead snake, taking a few deep breaths to calm himself. "Perhaps I should hire an investigator while I am in London," he suggested.

"Perhaps you should," the viscount replied. Then he added, "Let's get this thing out of here before any of the women see it."

John used the sword to lift the still body back into the box. He carried it toward the stables, accompanied by the viscount, and bade Brooks bury it. He kept the box's paper wrapping as evidence, thinking an investigator might appreciate the handwriting sample the address provided.

"We have to tell Willa," he told Yale. "She deserves to know, and she needs to be aware of every possible threat."

"I hate having to tell her," her father said.

"She's strong," John said. "Quite strong, and it is better to be aware than to be ignorant of something like this."

"We should include my wife and Fayre in the conversation, then," the viscount said. "We all need to be aware."

"Yes. It's close to dinner time. Let us leave it until afterwards. It is not much of a mealtime conversation."

"At the same time, we can tell them you will be going to London to seek both medical advice and an investigator."

"I may as well leave tomorrow, and will entrust Willa's safety to you while I am gone."

"I believe we can trust Abbott and Brooks as well, and most likely Molly. I will meet with them individually to talk to them about the threats."

Back in the house, John retired to his room to clean up and change for dinner. "Martin, I will be leaving for London on the morrow," John told his valet as the man assisted him into an evening jacket.

"Will I be going with you?" Martin asked.

"Not this time. It will be a fast trip and I can make do with one of the London servants for a few days."

"I shall pack for you, then."

"Not much, only a valise. I will be riding my horse and traveling light. Also, I do have a town wardrobe in London."

"Yes, my lord, you do at that. I will pack a few things for you this evening then."

"Thank you. I have another reason for not having you accompany me. I was wondering if, while I am gone for a few days, you would take the gig and return home to collect a bit more of a wardrobe for me. I do not intend to leave until my fiancée is recovered or we are married. I'm sure you are getting tired of cleaning the same items over and over."

The valet agreed. "It would be nice if we both had more extensive wardrobes."

"I'll write a letter to my mother this evening, and you can deliver it. Also, I'll write one for my estate manager."

"I will be happy to deliver them," Martin assured him.

Dinner was, as usual, delicious. The family sat together at one end of the long table, the viscountess at her husband's right side with her niece next to her. Willa sat to her father's left with John beside her. John had discovered dinner at the Amhearst estate was casual, and he was comfortable with it. He might be an earl, but he tried not to let his title go to his head. After all, he had inherited it from his father, whose own father had passed it on to him. He smiled fondly at Willa as she exclaimed over the roasted vegetables Cook had served with the perfectly roasted beef.

"I do love carrots," she said. "Perhaps I should have been a rabbit."

Fayre had laughed outright. "Your ears are not nearly big enough, cousin dear."

"I have never known a horse who was not fond of a carrot," John joked. "I can see you as a sleek and high-bred mare, far before I can a rabbit."

"Silly man," she replied.

The viscount, not to be left out of the fun, joined in. "My dear, I do believe John has a valid point. You are a fearless rider, so I suspect you would be quite a good horse."

"Do you remember how exhausted her nurse was when Willa was a toddler?" the viscountess asked her husband. "Our first nurse quit, and we had to hire a younger one." She swung her gaze from Yale to Willa, "I can certainly see you as a race horse."

The foolishness continued. John was thankful the conversation was light, and he was sure Lord Amhearst felt the same as the man seemed to encourage the continuation of the silliness. At last, after a pumpkin trifle, the small group retired to the drawing room where Abbott served them tea. The viscount cleared his throat to get their attention.

"We had an event today," he said, instantly gaining the rapt attention of all three women.

The viscountess, sounding suspicious, asked what type of event had happened.

"I'll be blunt," her husband said. "It was another attempt on Willa's life."

The sound of three feminine gasps filled the room. It was Willa who spoke next. "What happened? I didn't notice anything." Her eyes swung between her father and John.

"Abbott heard a knock at the door," her father explained. "When he answered, there was no one there, but a parcel addressed to you sat on the doorstep. He brought it into the library where John and I were sitting. John noticed immediately how the weight of the contents kept moving around in the box."

"Oh, dear, what was it?" Blythe asked.

John had lifted Willa from her Bath chair so she could be comfortable on the settee. He had then sat next to her. Reaching over, he now took her hand in his own before her father finished the telling of what had happened.

"There was a snake in the box, an adder."

"But those are poisonous," Fayre burst out. "Someone sent Willa a deadly snake?"

Willa's hand had tightened around John's; Blythe had turned pale. He hurried to assure them. "I dispatched it with your father's sword rather quickly," he told them, purposely failing to mention how the snake had struck his boot. "Please be assured he is not loose in the garden."

"It's true, then," Lady Amhearst said. "Someone is trying to kill our daughter."

"I'm afraid so," her husband agreed. "It leads me to an announcement which John and I have to make." He paused, before going on. "John will be leaving tomorrow to go to London."

Willa turned toward him, "Whatever for?"

"I'm going to seek out the advice of some physicians, a second opinion, as your father calls it. And I'm going to hire an investigator to come and look into who is trying to harm you."

"That will make me feel much better," the viscountess said.

"How long will you be gone?" Willa asked him.

"A sennight, perhaps," he replied. "I will be riding my horse and traveling light. If I leave at first light, I may well arrive before dark the next day. I will work quickly while I am in town. Your father knows of an investigator who has a good reputation. Therefore, I will visit him first so he can get started here if he is willing to take on the case. Then I intend to go to the Royal College of Physicians, Oxford, and Cambridge to speak to some knowledgeable physicians and find out what the most learned men of science know about spinal injuries."

"After John leaves tomorrow," Yale interjected, "I will speak with Abbott, Molly, and Brooks about making sure those few servants we can trust keep an eye out for your well-being and safety. I also want us all to be extra vigilant in the days to come."

"Yes," John said, lifting Willa's hand to his lips and brushing them gently across the back of it. "I am nervous about leaving you, Willa dear, but your father will keep you safe from harm while I am gone. Promise me you will be extra careful of your own safety and report any suspicious things to your father."

"I promise," she whispered.

Chapter Eleven

The trip to London went better than John expected. He left at first light and paced his horse on the road toward the city. Though traveling light just as he had claimed he would, he did arm himself on the chance a highwayman might present a threat to him. At lunch he stopped at an inn where he enjoyed a meat pie and a pint of ale, then he stopped at dark to let his horse rest and to get some sleep himself. It was the next afternoon when he arrived at his town house. Once there, he changed and cleaned up before leaving to visit the investigator.

The investigator's office smelled of tobacco. A young man sat at a desk in the outer office and soon escorted him into the inner office, introducing John to the investigator. Yale had filled John in on the man's credentials. Samuel Parker had left the Bow Street Runners just a few years earlier after suffering from a gunshot wound to the shoulder. Now, John greeted the other man. "I have heard a lot about you, Mr. Parker. Lord Amhearst has nothing but the best to say about you."

"The respect is mutual," the investigator said. "The viscount is a good man. Now, what I can do for you, Lord Roydon?"

John took a seat when Mr. Parker indicated he should do so. "I am affianced to the viscount's only daughter."

Mr. Parker smiled. "Congratulations! When are the nuptials?"

"They were scheduled for a short time before the holiday, but we were forced to postpone them."

"Oh?"

"Miss Dutton had a riding accident and it is feared she suffers from paralysis."

The man's face displayed sympathy. "That is most regrettable. Is there no hope for her?"

"We're unsure," John answered. "One of my intents during my visit to town is to seek the advice of the most renowned physicians." John was quiet for a moment. "The reason I came to you is because the viscount and I are sure someone is trying to harm Miss Dutton, possibly even to kill her."

Mr. Parker reached for a pen and tablet. "Tell me what gives you this idea."

"The day of the accident, the saddle girth strap had been cut almost through. When Willa, that is Miss Dutton, and her horse started to take a fence, a bird flew up and hit the horse in the belly. The groom reports Miss Dutton and the saddle flew off the horse. She fell and struck a tree root."

John paused as the man scribbled notes and then looked back up from his writing. "Do go on, my lord."

Continuing with the recounting, John outlined the approximate timeline. When John finished telling Mr. Parker of the incidents in the stables and in the house, the investigator looked up at him. "Do you have any idea who would wish to do Miss Dutton harm?"

"Unfortunately, no one comes to mind. I did wonder if perhaps the culprit is trying to get some type of revenge on Lord Amhearst. In his business, I'm sure he has made enemies over the years."

The investigator scribbled a note. "Does anyone in particular come to his mind?"

"No. He agrees that, over the years, he has made enemies, but no one who displayed this level of anger."

"And you, Lord Roydon, do you have any enemies who might be wishing to harm your fiancée?"

"I can think of no one," John admitted.

John watched as the investigator read over his notes again. "It seems to me last spring there was talk about a young woman blackmailing another to marry you."

John looked intently at the investigator. "Yes, there was. Willa's cousin, Miss Claire Stuart, was attacked by Viscount Pitt. After witnessing the attack his sister, Lady Regina Norton, blackmailed Miss Stuart during the season. In fact, that is how Miss Dutton and I met. My friend, the Duke of Lamberton met Miss Stuart and immediately became enamored of her. However, her attentions for him ran hot and cold until she finally confessed she was being blackmailed. At that time, Lady Norton was caught in an indelicate situation and backed off of the threats."

"Is that how it ended, then?"

"Afterward, Lady Norton did start to spread rumors around London. Lamberton took care of it by visiting with the girl's father. It was discovered she was with child and her father sent her to Yorkshire to live with an aunt. I can't imagine any threat is left there. Besides, she didn't want to marry me."

"Hmm," the other man sounded thoughtful. Parker scribbled more on his notepad and then looked up at John. "I will take the case and start right away. I'll skulk around town a bit tomorrow, and then I'll tool out to the Amhearst's estate."

"I appreciate it. I am to assure you that you can be a guest of the Amhearst's as long as necessary. If you should arrive there before I do, the viscount will answer more questions. They are presently waiting to receive back reference checks on the newer staff."

"Wonderful."

After a discussion about payment, John rose to take his leave and bade the investigator a good day before leaving the office with a sense of satisfaction. As it was late in the day, he retired to his home where the staff had been thrown into a tizzy at his unexpected arrival. It was obvious the cook had sent scullery maids and footmen scurrying hither and thither, and she had put together a respectable evening meal. John dined on turbot served with a rich sauce and several side dishes before retiring to the library where he sat beside the fire and contemplated his next day's activities. He hoped he had as much success in seeking second opinions as he had with hiring an investigator. Knowing Willa might be paralyzed for the rest of her life made his heart ache.

❧

The days without John stretched by for Willa. On the first day, she spent time listening to Fayre practice the pianoforte. Willa read and then, out of desperation, picked up her needlework only to take a few stitches before having to untangle a knot in the floss and then pick out several more.

The next day, she begged her father to take her out to see Pirate. Willa fed him an apple and a carrot and saw a gleam in his darks eyes brought on by the extra special treatment. The viscount didn't want her to spend too much time outside after the last attempt to harm her. Without asking, Willa wondered if he was worried someone might take a shot at her. At least it would put her out of her misery fast, she realized.

Day three brought a bit of relief when the vicar stopped by to call on them. Lady Amhearst and Fayre had gone into the village, so Willa entertained him alone. "I'm so happy you stopped in," she told him as they waited for tea to be served. "I was about to send a note to you, asking you to visit."

"Oh, well then, this is exceptional timing, is it not?" Vicar Wright had settled into a seat near her Bath chair. "Is there something you wanted to talk to me about?"

"Yes, there is," Willa decided to get right to the point. "I am contemplating releasing the earl from our engagement."

The vicar was silent for a bit and then replied, "Might I ask why?"

"I'm suffering from paralysis, Vicar Wright. It is a lifelong affliction, and John deserves a whole woman to be his wife. Dr. Saunders has told me I dare not risk having a child. John deserves and needs an heir. I cannot walk anywhere. I cannot stand up by myself. I cannot even move myself from my bed to my chair. I am ridiculously helpless, and I love him so much I am realizing he deserves more."

"I see what you are saying," the man spoke softly as the butler entered with the tea tray. Abbott arranged the tray on the table, and Willa realized she was not even able to reach the pot of tea to pour. "Please pour for us, Abbott."

"As you wish, Miss." When the tea, biscuits, and finger sandwiches had been served, the butler bowed and quietly left the room, leaving the door ajar.

"This was a perfect example, Vicar. I cannot even get myself close enough to the tea tray to play the role of hostess. John is an earl and a well-respected one; he needs a hostess. And while his mother is healthy and may be willing to continue to serve in the role, she shouldn't need to. That should be his wife's duty."

"So you love him enough to release him?"

"Yes, I do. After all, almost anyone else would make him a better wife. Our dinner party is a fine example. Miss Marty is perfect for him. The two enjoy the same activities, seem to converse easily on endless topics, and she is a wonderful woman who also deserves to marry a nice gentleman."

"Have you spoken to your fiancé about this?" the vicar asked her.

"No. He's such a gentleman he would argue I should not break our engagement on these grounds."

"And if you come to this decision for sure, what will you do if he refuses?"

"I plan to prove I am right. I will show him how he needs a normal wife, not someone like me. I've been contemplating playing a bit of a matchmaker. If Miss Marty is not ideal for him, I will convince my parents to host a house party, and I will parade eligible young women in front of him."

"I see. And what will you do if he does accept your offer and proposes to someone else?"

Willa felt tears pool in her eyes. "I'm not sure. The truth is, Vicar Wright, there aren't many options open for me. Although my father's title will pass to his cousin's oldest son, I know my father will assure my financial comfort. Of course I will need to move from the estate someday, but I will be able to afford a town home in Bath or a cottage somewhere. There will be no point in having land as I cannot ride a horse." Here the tears began to slide down her cheeks. "I just don't know what I will do for my mental activity." Willa fell silent before setting her tea cup onto a nearby side table with a clatter. "I am so bored, I don't know what to do with myself," she admitted.

The vicar set down his own cup and leaned forward to take her hand in his and pat the back of it comfortingly. "I will pray for you, Miss Willa. I will pray you make the right decisions for everyone involved. Particularly, I will pray you find a purpose in your new life, something you can be at peace with."

❧

It was five days later, soon after sundown when John rode through the gates of the Amhearst estate. He was tired and beaten down. John had talked to several of the renowned men of medicine and had a promise from one young physician who was considered to be a forward-thinking man to come within a few days. Otherwise, the news had not been good. Little was known about spinal injuries. For those who suffered from them, there was little hope.

A groom ran out to take the reins of his horse as John rode into the stable yard. Soon, Willa's own groom stepped outside as well. "Welcome back, my lord"

"Thank you, Brooks. I must say it is good to dismount." Indeed, he was happy to set his feet on the ground. "Has anything untoward happened in my absence?"

"No, my lord, it has been unusually quiet. Miss Willa came out twice to visit Pirate, accompanied by her father. Otherwise, she has been housebound, I believe. A visitor has arrived. A Mr. Samuel Parker from London."

"Yes, I had heard he planned on visiting the estate. I'll leave my horse in your good care and make my way up to the house. If I hurry, I may be in time for dinner."

Indeed, the door swung open as John stepped up to it. How Abbott knew someone had arrived, he would always wonder. "Abbott," he greeted the butler. "Am I in time for dinner?"

"Yes, my lord, and I believe you have time to change."

John chuckled. "Is that your discreet way of telling me I smell like horse and am covered with road dust?"

"I would never suggest it, my lord," Abbott replied with a sniff.

John found his valet in his room readying his evening wear. "Good evening, Martin," he said. "I see you expected me."

"Yes, my lord. One of the maids saw you coming down the road, and the news has spread like wildfire."

"Ah! It has always been a mystery to me how all the staff seem to know things so quickly. Now I know."

Martin's lips quirked. "Perhaps I should not say this, but we often know more about you than you do yourself."

John laughed. "That is what I fear!"

"I trust you had a productive trip, my lord."

"I'm not sure, but I do have a young physician who is well renowned coming in the next few days to give us a second opinion on Miss Willa's condition."

"That is good. I still pray for her every night. Miss Willa is such a delightful young lady and well thought of by the staff."

The two fell quiet as John readied himself for dinner. After making his way downstairs to the drawing room where he found his fiancée, her cousin, and her parents visiting with Mr. Parker. The family all smiled at him as he walked in the door.

"John, you are back," Willa said. He strode across the room and bent to brush a discreet kiss across her cheek, wishing they did not always have an audience.

"And am glad to be so," he told her in return before taking the seat closest to her Bath chair.

"How did it go, John?" Yale asked him.

John would not say anything to dash any hope Willa might have. He would talk to her parents alone. "A young physician by the name of Dr. Lead will be here within a few days. He is renowned in the Royal College of Physicians and at Oxford where he studied."

"What did the others say?" the viscountess asked.

John answered quickly so as not to give them time to assume he was prevaricating. "Not a lot is known about spinal injuries."

Thankfully, he was interrupted by the butler who announced dinner. John stood and reached for the handles of Willa's chair to wheel her in. "I missed you," he said quietly. "How were the days I was gone?"

"Long, John. The days were so long. Of course, Papa will not let me leave the house, even to sit in the garden, unless he is with me. I saw Pirate twice, but otherwise have been restricted to indoors."

John found his heart often felt heavy for Willa. He resolved to put some thought into helping her with more independence. The injury was chafing on her and he was well aware of it. First though, they had to find out who was trying to kill her, for he believed it was her death they sought.

Dinner was spent amicably, and when the ladies withdrew to the parlour, John spoke up. "I hear things have been quiet here since I left."

"Yes, they have been," Yale spoke as he lit a cheroot. "Mr. Parker is keeping a low profile but talking to all the servants and stable hands, as well as spending time in the village."

"It's surprising what you can sometimes learn over an ale in an inn, but I admit to having found nothing outside of the estate," the investigator said.

"What is your story? Who do the servants believe you to be?"

"I am a lover of horseflesh who is visiting to learn as much as I can from the famous Lord Amhearst about breeding bloodstock."

"Ah," John nodded, "that is a good one. Quite believable."

"It also gives him an excuse to spend a lot of time in the stables, since that is where the threats began."

"And have you learned anything at all?"

"I have found several people I do not think are guilty. Miss Dutton is well thought of, and many of the older retainers and even the newer servants are extremely loyal. However, there are a few that, while they do not openly display any hostility toward her, also do not display any loyalty. I am concentrating my efforts on looking into them at this time."

Yale chuckled, "He has also been cozying up with Cook, making trips to the kitchens to compliment her and to ask for receipts for his own household."

"Yes, by doing so I can slip in a question now and then about staff. And Abbott, knowing of the threats, is willing to speak to me about the household staff as well. Again, I have ruled several people out, such as Miss Dutton's maid, Molly, but I have not ruled out everyone."

The viscount looked at John then and said, "You were a bit evasive about what you found out about Willa's condition."

"Yes, I didn't want to say anything in front of her. The men offered little hope. It doesn't mean there isn't any, it simply means that little is known about it. Dr. Lead is interested in meeting her and examining her, he said something about swelling around the spinal cord, but it is the most hope I received."

"I do admit I had hoped for more," Yale replied. "It is breaking my heart to see my daughter in this condition."

"I understand. I, too, had hoped for a miracle. As I rode back, I thought it may be time to move past this stage of hoping and move to how to make her more independent and satisfied with her condition. Willa is such a lively person that being restrained to a cumbersome chair on wheels is hard on her."

"It certainly is."

Mr. Parker spoke up. "If I may make a suggestion, I wonder if perhaps, her Bath chair might be modified so she could push the wheels herself. Miss Dutton might not be able to do so for any distance, but perhaps within a room she could get around a bit more independently. I have noticed you have two Bath chairs, so she could do with one until someone adjusts the other."

John and Yale both swung their gazes to the investigator. John replied thoughtfully, "I see what you mean. If the wheels were set farther forward on the chair, she could reach down and propel herself forward."

Yale's face brightened. "I have my own blacksmith, and he is quite good with what he does. I think we should speak to him tomorrow, John, to see if he has any ideas of how to improve the design."

"Also, you might be able to have him build a type of lifting device which would allow her to lift herself in and out of bed. It could be hung from a beam over her bed and involve a canvas seat and a lifting bar."

Again the men looked at him in astonishment. "Mr. Parker," the viscount said, "you should have been an engineer."

The other man chuckled. "I do admit I thought about it but knew I would need to attend university, and schooling has never been something I enjoyed."

"I can't wait to look into these suggestions more," John said.

"Yes," Yale agreed, "let's speak to the blacksmith early in the morning. Then, if we feel he has any ideas, I'll let you approach Willa with them. After all, you will need to make the same modifications in your own home when you are married."

Chapter Twelve

John and Yale ate an early and hearty breakfast before leaving the house to talk to the blacksmith. The two of them told Abbott they were taking the downstairs Bath chair with them. The butler would get one of the footmen to carry Willa downstairs and another to bring the other chair down to the first floor. They pushed the chair down to the smithy and stepped under the roof of the shed to interrupt his work.

"Morning, my lords," he said, obviously surprised at the visit. "How can I help ye?"

"Lord Roydon and I need your opinion, Dawson," the viscount began. "Miss Willa is having to use a Bath chair for mobility now that she is suffering from paralysis, and we were wondering what you might be able to do to improve it."

The blacksmith looked out at the chair, squinting in the morning sunlight. Dawson laid down the piece of iron he had in his hand, stripped off his heavy gloves, and walked over to the chair where he squatted down and began to inspect it. John and Yale watched as he walked around it, pushed and pulled it, and tested the seat with his hand. The blacksmith took off his cap and ran his hand through his hair, put it back on, and then turned to look at them.

"The first thing I would recommend is for me to remove this hood. Does she need it? Sure, it would keep the sun off her face, but I see her outside, and she always wears a hat."

John stepped closer as understanding dawned. "If the hood were removed, she would be able to reach the wheels and propel them forward at least a short distance without needing someone to always push or pull it."

"That's right," Dawson said. "Then, if it were up to me, I'd cut off this foot rest and put on a smaller one. Most women's feet ain't big enough to need much space." The blacksmith indicated the steering mechanism and the front foot support. "I can cut down the steering handle and the undercarriage support and move the front wheel back. That would make it a good bit shorter in length and easier to handle."

Yale looked at John. "I was sure he would be able to fix it. What do you think?"

"We should let him," John said decisively.

The viscount looked back at his employee. "Do it Dawson. Unless a horse urgently needs shoeing, make it a priority."

"I will, my lord."

"The other thing is," Lord Amhearst continued, "please put some thought into a type of lifting device. Something which attaches to the beam in the ceiling which would allow my daughter to lift herself from the chair to her bed without always needing help."

The blacksmith nodded. "Maybe with a canvas sling she can put underneath herself and something for her hands to use to lift her body with? Then it would swing to either side?"

"Yes, that is what I had in mind," the viscount said.

"I'll do it. I'll muse on it, and after I'm done with the chair here, I'll sketch out some ideas."

"Thank you," the viscount said.

"Yes, Dawson, your help is much appreciated," John added before joining the viscount to stroll to the house.

Once inside the house, Yale turned to John. "I have some estate business to see to. Would you like to tell Willa what the plan is?"

"I will," John said. Then he asked Abbott, "Where is Miss Willa this morning?"

"She is in the morning parlour, my lord."

John walked into the room and saw Willa sitting there alone, a pot of tea on a center table nowhere near where she sat. "Good morning. Are you alone?"

Willa turned and smiled, "For the moment."

John walked over and used one finger to tilt her chin up. He covered her mouth with his, deepening the kiss as she sighed, breaking off only when footsteps sounded nearby. "You and I are not alone enough," he murmured as he straightened.

"Good morning, John," Fayre said as she bustled in, a book in her hands.

"Good morning, Fayre," he greeted the young woman as he took a seat close to Willa. "What are you two doing this morning?"

"We were going to read a chapter in a book we are enjoying and share tea," Willa told him. "Fayre forgot the book, and I got distracted by watching the squirrels outside the window, and my tea grew cold. I suspect the entire pot is cold and we should ring for another."

Fayre jumped back up from her seat and touched the pot. "Oh, yes, it is." She moved to the door where she summoned a nearby footman and made the request.

John looked over at Willa's cup. It was empty, although there was some moisture in the bottom. "Your cup is empty, though," he stated the obvious.

Willa looked at him. "Only because I cannot even move when I am alone in this chair. I was tired of balancing it so I wouldn't spill it while laughing at the squirrels, so I dumped the cold tea in the only available place – the houseplant." Indeed there was a flowering plant sitting on a plant stand next to her chair. "It needed watering anyway, and Claire always insists tea is good for plants."

"Claire would know," John agreed. "I will admit I saw Noel putting tea grounds and egg shells on his plants as well."

John reached across to take Willa's hand. "I have good news for you, then."

"What is it?" Willa asked. Fayre's attention had turned to him, too.

"Your father and I took one of the Bath chairs out to visit with Dawson, the blacksmith."

"So that is why the footman had to carry the upstairs chair down for me."

"Yes. We asked Dawson if there was anything he might do to make it better for you." John chuckled, "I'd call it a monstrosity as it is now."

"It is," Willa agreed. "The chair is as big as a sofa."

"Well, he is going to remove the hood so you can reach over the edge and propel the wheels forward if you would like. It's heavy, so I don't expect you will be able to push it too far without tiring, but I also know you are quite strong for a woman."

"Ah, so I could push it over to the teapot, for instance."

"That will be wonderful for you, Willa," Fayre chimed in.

"It's better than just that, though," John said. "Dawson's going to cut down the foot rest and shorten the steering handle, moving the front wheel back so it will be quite a bit shorter in length. When he is done you will even be able to sit at a table and be close enough to reach it."

Willa looked thoughtful, "Will he do it to both chairs?"

"Yes, but one at a time. That way if it doesn't work well, we can replace the one and still have a workable chair until the replacement arrives."

A maid came in and set down a fresh tea tray, quietly removing the other and leaving the room. Fayre rose to pour and handed Willa and John each a cup before pouring one for herself.

"Not that I mind pushing Willa around in the chair, but this will surely make her much more independent."

"Your uncle and I feel so," John said. Turning back to Willa, he continued. "We also asked Dawson to design a device to be mounted above your bed which would allow you to swing yourself from the bed to the chair. Even that bit would help. It would allow you to move back into your own room but still keep the door locked against threats until we have solved the problem of who is trying to harm you."

"Hmm. Dawson is good at what he does. It will be interesting to see what he comes up with. Speaking of which, has Mr. Parker made any headway that you know of?"

"Parker is interviewing all the employees in great detail. We should also hear back from the reference checks soon," he added. "Until then, of course, we all have to continue to be vigilant. I assume nothing untoward has happened since the snake was delivered."

"No," Willa said. "Although I must always watch my back. It is making me edgy."

"It is making me angry," John replied. "Infuriated, in fact. I cannot imagine why anyone would wish to harm you. Willa, you are the most wonderful woman in the world."

❧

The most wonderful woman in the world, Willa mused later in the night as she lay in bed next to a sleeping Fayre. She tried to roll over, forgetting momentarily how she was unable to move her legs and then flopped back down on her back, frustrated. Willa loved John so much, and knowing she had to let him go made her heart ache. John had spent the afternoon with her, taking her on a walk to see Pirate and then to sit in the garden sheltered from the cool breeze. Indeed, he had talked to her about the things he wanted to do to make her more independent – fix the Bath chair, make a lift for her so she was able to get out of bed and into the chair without help, remodel one of the rooms at his home so their bed chamber would be on the ground floor, put in ramps at each door to the outside. It didn't matter, though. Willa still would never be the wife he needed, and she had to release him. The time was drawing near.

Since she could not sleep, Willa struggled with how she would let him go. John was an honourable man, and she knew he would not easily accept her offer to release him. Many men would do so readily, in fact with much relief. John would not. She decided she would need to give him a nudge, a shove even toward Marty Robinson. While Miss Marty wasn't quite as highly ranked, she was still a member of the ton. Miss Marty was near John's age, yet still young enough to give him a healthy heir.

Willa was not sure how the two felt about each other. She knew John found Marty interesting. He would grow to be fond of her with time, surely. Marty might have feelings for John, but she was far too well bred to let them show, at least to Willa. Pondering this, Willa came to a decision just before her eyes slid shut in slumber. She would host the house party she had thought about. Marty would be invited as well as other eligible young women so John had a choice.

The ladies in the Amhearst household were used to breaking their fast alone. The viscount and the earl were often out in the stables, talking to the workers, checking on the horses, and even exercising their steeds by the time Willa, Fayre, and Lady Amhearst sat around the table eating and sipping on chocolate or tea. The morning after Willa made her decision about the house party was no different. Willa lifted a piece of crisp bacon to her mouth, nibbled at it, and then looked across the table to her mother.

"Mother," she ventured, "you know I am bored beyond belief."

"Yes, dear, and I'm sorry about that. Unfortunately, you were never a girl who took to needlework or something you could more easily accomplish now. Instead, you insisted on tagging after your father through the stables far too much. I'm sorry now that I ever allowed it."

Willa shrugged, "Don't be. At least I have those fond memories. I did wonder if you and Papa would allow me to host a little house party."

Fayre looked up with interest. "Wouldn't it be fun?"

Blythe, too, looked up with interest. "That would be fun, and you did an excellent job of hosting the dinner party. It would most certainly break up the tedium you experience. Who would you invite?"

"I haven't decided yet. I wanted your permission first. I did plan to concentrate on young women about my age. Then we could invite more of the neighbors in for the activities, as well, without having to house them. Perhaps just a sennight, since we are getting closer and closer to the holidays."

"Yes, and we could host it right away. There are not many activities this time of year, and I'm sure the mothers of the girls who didn't take during the season would be happy to have a second chance for their daughters to meet an eligible bachelor. I assume you will be inviting a few of them, too."

"Of course," Willa agreed. "What would a house party be without equal numbers?"

"I'll speak to your father about it as soon as he has returned to the house," her mother promised. "Why don't you and Fayre make tentative plans by then? I am sure we can cajole him into agreeing. And John will be a strong advocate. He is worried about you and wishes to make your life more pleasant."

Poor man, Willa mused. John had no idea it was all for his benefit.

After breakfast, Willa asked Fayre if she would wheel her into the morning parlour. They would need paper and pen, she pointed out, and the small desk there would have all they needed. The door to the room stood open, the morning sun pouring through the east facing windows and beckoning them as they approached. Fayre guided Willa through the door and pushed her toward the same place she had sat the day before. Willa looked toward her favorite plant and her breath caught in her chest. The leaves were withered, the plant drooping. The plant had little life left in it. Willa was confused and then remembered the tea. She had dumped a cup of tea on the plant just twenty-four hours earlier. Tea had never hurt a plant in the past. While she didn't frequently dump her tea on plants, Claire did it all the time. So did Noel, as did many people. What would cause this? Unless . . .

"Go get Abbott, Fayre. Now, please."

Fayre did as she was bade and soon the butler entered the room, "You asked for me, Miss Willa?"

"Yes. Do you know what might have happened to this plant?"

The man looked to the plant she indicated, "No, it was healthy just yesterday." Abbott walked ahead and fingered the now dead leaves. "I haven't a clue."

That was what she feared. "Do you have any idea where Mr. Parker is? Or my father or the earl?"

"Lord Amhearst and the earl are both out, no doubt in the stables. I will send for them. Mr. Parker is meeting with the housekeeper. I will fetch him immediately." Most likely sensing the urgency in her voice, he bustled away.

"What do you think happened?" Fayre asked.

"I do believe someone tried to poison me yesterday by putting something in my tea. The tea which grew cold and that I dumped onto the plant."

Fayre sank onto a nearby chair. "Oh no," she whispered. "I am so frightened for you, Willa. Why would anyone do this?"

A few moments later Mr. Parker entered the room, "Miss Dutton," he greeted her.

"Mr. Parker," Willa began, "yesterday morning Fayre and I came into this room as is our morning habit. We normally spend a bit of time reading a book aloud to each other so we both might enjoy it. However, we forgot the book yesterday. Right after our tea was served and Fayre had poured it, she went to get the book. Meanwhile, two squirrels outside the window were playfully chasing each other, and I grew distracted, allowing my tea to grow cold. In fact, I was laughing so hard my tea began to slosh a bit, so I wanted to pour it out. The only thing close enough, since I cannot move this chair, was this plant. Yesterday it was healthy, but look at it, Mr. Parker."

Willa could almost feel the man thinking. "And you did not drink even a sip of the tea?" he asked.

"No, nary a sip. Neither did Fayre, as hers was also cold by the time she returned with the book."

"What happened to the tea?"

"After the earl joined us, we had a maid deliver another pot, and she removed the cold tea."

A flurry of activity could be heard, and Willa's father, John, and her mother soon all burst into the room. "What has happened?" John demanded of Mr. Parker, his jaw clenched and his fists tight.

Mr. Parker looked at John. "I assume you remember the tea from yesterday morning," he said.

"Yes, it was cold and Willa told me she dumped it on the plant." At that, his gaze followed the investigator's to the plant. "It's dead," John stated the obvious.

"There is only one thing I can think of which might be meant to kill a human but will also kill a plant. Arsenic."

❧

The word ran over and over in John's mind. Someone had tried to kill Willa again. As the thought became clearer in his mind, he spoke without thinking of the impact of his words. "That means they were willing to kill Fayre as well."

That young woman made a squealing sound at the words and grew pale. "I'm sorry," John uttered. "I didn't mean to upset you, Fayre."

"But it's true," she replied. "I, too, was to drink the tea unless it was just in Willa's cup. I don't think that could be," she said as she rose and paced. "I poured the tea, not the maid. There is no way anyone could have known which cup I would give to my cousin. Furthermore, isn't arsenic a powder?" Here she stopped and looked to Mr. Parker until the man nodded and murmured his agreement. "I am sure there was nothing in either cup," she continued. "Mother taught me to always look, in case there should be a small bug or something."

John became aware of the viscountess shutting the door. "We must send Fayre home, so she is not at risk," Lady Amhearst stated.

"No," Fayre replied adamantly. "I am here to help. The more eyes we have to watch, the less likely something is to happen. I will not be sent home because of a single threat against me when poor Willa has faced so many already."

"I appreciate it," Willa said. "Sometimes Fayre is all that keeps me sane, the only thing which keeps me from worrying about my own life all the time. And without her in the bed at night, I would not be safe because we would have to leave the door unlocked. I would not even be able to get to the bell pull to summon help without her."

"You're right," the viscount entered into the conversation. "We do need Fayre." Yale turned toward Mr. Parker, "Have you any leads yet?"

"I believe I have it down to two possibilities in the stable. I am waiting to hear back on our reference checks. In the house, the only person I am watchful of is the nurse. However, I am mostly basing it on her being the newest employee, and it is not fair to do so. We should hear back on her reference checks soon."

"We cannot wait much longer to act," John put in. "We must do so without delay."

Chapter Thirteen

The next day a well-respected young physician arrived at the estate. He was introduced to Willa as Dr. Lead. Since he arrived shortly before tea, he did not do an examination right away. Instead, after John and the viscount joined them for tea, the doctor asked them all about how she had been found at the scene of the accident, the position in which she was lying, and the location of where her back had hit the tree roots. Then he moved on to the level of pain she had experienced.

"Right after the accident it was quite bad but still tolerable without laudanum," Willa told him.

"Am I to understand that it has decreased somewhat?" he asked her.

Willa contemplated her answer. "Yes, yes it has," she replied. "It is always present, but tolerable. More like a dull ache I only notice when I concentrate on it. There was a storm recently, and it did flare up that night. In fact, it was bad enough I agreed to be dosed with laudanum."

"When you go upstairs to prepare for dinner, I would like to examine you if you will agree to it. Of course, I would also like to speak with your maid and your nurse, so let us make sure they are present."

Consequently, Willa had John carry her up to her room a bit earlier than usual. Molly and Nancy assisted her in unrobing and, as Dr. Lead asked, she was laid on her bed, face down in only her chemise. While Willa suffered from minor embarrassment as she was rather quite exposed to the doctor despite his efforts to be discreet, she did feel he was thorough. He tested at what point she lost sensation. Dr. Lead ran his hands down her spine, he examined it for abnormalities and any remaining bruising. At the completion of that, she was rolled over by Nancy and Molly, and the physician moved her legs, tested them for feeling, and afterwards moved on to her feet. At last he stood back.

"I will take my leave now, Miss Dutton, and let your maids prepare you for dinner."

"What is your diagnosis?" she asked him with a small amount of hope in her heart.

"I am going to review the information tonight. I will tell you in the morning."

"That must mean I am forced yet again to be patient," she mumbled to herself.

John and her family, too, seemed anxious to hear the physician's opinion, for they questioned him at dinner. He held firm, however, and refused to speak of it until he had time to muse upon it. The night seemed long as a result. Willa laid next to her sleeping cousin and realized how long each day seemed to stretch. She had decided not to speak to John about releasing him until she found what the doctor had decided, but she would need to do so soon.

Not long before he took his leave, Dr. Lead asked for her fiancé and her family to gather. Once they were all in the drawing room, he spoke.

"Unfortunately, we do not understand much about spinal injuries. We do occasionally see a miraculous recovery, but I am not sure we can count on that for Miss Dutton. That doesn't mean it won't happen, it simply means you should prepare for the paralysis to last a lifetime."

It was John who asked what Willa wished to but was afraid of the answer. "What about children? Dr. Saunders said she dare not risk it."

"I would not rush it, in case there is a chance of recovery. Pregnancy can put stress on the body at the best of times. With a spinal injury, if it were something like spinal swelling, a pregnancy might severely exacerbate it. However, once a year or so has passed, certainly there is no reason why she could not carry one or two children to full term and deliver healthy babies. You would, of course, require a nursemaid to assist with them, but it is to be expected in any case."

After the doctor bade them all goodbye and was escorted to the door by John and Lord and Lady Amhearst, a footman arrived almost immediately with the Bath chair. It had been cut down and remodeled, and Willa was thrilled. Sitting in it she could now propel it forward or backward by pushing the wheels with her hands. The only thing she noticed was how it irritated the tender skin of her palms. Looking up at Fayre she said, "Would you mind running upstairs to fetch one of my older pairs of kid gloves? If Molly is there, she will be familiar with which pairs I wear for every day."

"Of course," Fayre said as she leapt up and left the room quickly.

"Should we have Dawson adjust the other chair in the same manner?" her father asked.

"My first reaction is yes, but to be sure, let's give me until tomorrow to decide."

Nancy, who had been summoned for a few words with Dr. Lead about Willa's care before he left, spoke up. "If I may say so Miss, it is a good idea. You may find trying to push yourself around becomes too exhausting for you, though."

"I doubt it," Willa replied. "I am strong and will develop more strength by doing so, but I will wait until tomorrow."

Nancy curtsied and slipped from the room just as Fayre returned, holding out a pair of soft, gray leather gloves. "These are the ones Molly said are the oldest but still in good condition."

After slipping them on, Willa discovered propelling the chair was much easier. Willa smiled up at them all, needing time alone to go over what the physician had said, as well as her thoughts about John and their engagement. "Perfect," she said. "Now, if you don't mind, I would like to be alone to practice wheeling this about a bit. If I should need help, I will call for Abbott."

As they all left the room, albeit reluctantly, Willa did indeed practice moving around the room. It was work, especially turning, as she had to adjust the steering handle and then move her arms back to the wheels. But she was successful, and she would not again be unable to move at all when alone. As she remembered the attempted poisoning, she once again became angry about her situation. She forced her now-tired arms to move the chair to the window where she could look out upon the beautiful countryside while contemplating her future.

Less than an hour had passed when Willa came to a firm decision. She would release John and would play matchmaker to her own fiancé before telling him. Then, when he had come to realize she was a poor choice compared to a woman who could walk, dance, and ride, she would have a heart-to-heart talk with him and bow out of their relationship. Her parents would be stuck with her forever, but she was sure they would not mind so much. As soon as she had made up her mind, she wheeled over to the door and leaned forward to open it. Abbott was posted outside the door, listening for any calls of distress.

"Can I help you, Miss Willa?" he inquired with fond formality.

"Yes, I was wondering if you would send for my cousin. We are going to have a small house party just as soon as it can be arranged. It is imperative we begin our planning now."

❦

John had been secretly glad when Willa had dismissed them all. He walked out to the stables and demanded Pirate be saddled. After swinging up on Willa's horse's back, he rode out of the paddock and headed for open land. He needed to let his mind go over all the doctor had said.

As the wind rushed past him and Pirate seized the opportunity to run at a full gallop, John realized how angry he was. John was beyond furious for Willa and for himself. While he loved her like he had never cared for any woman, it angered him that she could no longer walk, or dance, or ride. Willa had a thirst for life many young women did not and because of a nameless, faceless assailant, she could no longer enjoy those things in life. They could no longer enjoy them together. And to know one of her fondest wishes – to become a mother – should be postponed made his heart ache. Indeed, as an earl he needed an heir. While it was not that important to him, it was his duty, and it might be questionable if Willa could provide one for him. He had to find out who was attempting to harm her and bring the perpetrator to justice. He remembered when his friend Noel had put an end to the man who was threatening Claire. John likewise had a desire to put a bullet in the person trying to harm his fiancée.

An hour later, Pirate was running out of steam, and John was ready to return to the estate. John pulled an apple from the basket of kitchen rejects and fed it to the horse as Brooks removed the tack and groomed the horse. Then John strode to the house and found Willa and Fayre busy in the drawing room. He kissed Willa on the cheek and smiled at Fayre as he settled into a chair near Willa.

"How did the wheeling practice go?"

"Good," she replied. "The gloves do help a lot, and I need to gain strength in my arms, but I will eventually need no one else to push me."

"We'll have Dawson do the same thing to the other chair if you still like it tomorrow. And then we'll have him get to work on a lifting device."

"That would be nice," Willa said

"What are you two ladies doing this morning?" Fayre had paper and pen and sat at a small escritoire. Willa was nearby.

"My cousin and I are planning a house party," came his fiancée's reply. "It is time I have a bit more of a social life, and this seems like a good way to start."

"Who will you invite?" he asked.

"I will keep it small with only 15 guests who will stay. That is all the room we have, and it includes some sharing, although I know those invited won't object. Then I will ask some of the neighbors in as well for certain events." Willa fell silent and then looked up. "I am inviting your particular friends, the Earl and Countess of Tabor."

That was good. Thomas was about his age and his younger wife Melinda was a delight to spend time with. "I appreciate it. Who else?"

"I have selected three young women who have not taken yet. With such short notice it might insure their acceptance. Miss Grace Clarke and her parents, Miss Kathryn Matthews and her aunt, Miss Lucinda Matthews, and Miss Caroline Russell and her parents."

John had a difficult time placing them. "Who are Miss Clarke's parents?"

"The Earl and Countess of Baddock. And Miss Russell's are the Baron and Baroness Macey."

"Ah," he nodded in recognition. "I am acquainted with the Baron as he is almost always in town, so hard is his wife trying to fire off their daughter. I have only met the Earl a few times this past season."

"Yes, this was Miss Clarke's first season, as it was mine."

"Well then, she cannot be as wonderful as you or she would have taken right away."

Willa laughed, "She is quite nice, but unfortunately her father is not wealthy and is somewhat of a known gambler. In fact, I thought twice about inviting them. No doubt he will be begging my father to offer horse racing so he can place a bet on the outcome. Then I decided I cannot take it out on poor Miss

Clarke. So instead, I have added Mr. Henry Hart to the invitation list. Mr. Hart inherited a fortune and both his parents are deceased so he must miss having a family. Furthermore, he has three younger sisters and no doubt needs the assistance in raising them."

John chuckled. His beloved was playing matchmaker, he noted. "Do go on with the list," he prompted.

Willa continued, "I am inviting the Earl of Shelton as he is a friend of yours and, quite frankly, it is time he settled."

John did not argue, knowing Shelton was looking for a wife, if only half-heartedly.

"The Viscount Gage and Mr. William Webster will round out my list of younger gentlemen, but I am also inviting Mr. Donald Miller as there has been much gossip about his interest in Miss Matthews' aunt, Miss Lucinda Matthews, who always accompanies her. Mr. Miller, as you no doubt are aware, is a widower with a good half dozen children who need a mother."

"Ah yes, I remember hearing that," John remarked. He waited patiently until she spoke again.

"Locally, I will invite much of the same group which came to dinner recently. Except for Mr. Patton. While I dearly love him, a party might be too much activity for him, although we may throw our numbers off and have him come for one of the dinners. Everyone finds him most entertaining, particularly the gentlemen."

"Yes, he is. I enjoyed his stories the night of the dinner party."

"Now Fayre and I are planning the activities," Willa said.

"Perhaps you should have a horse race," John prompted. "For the men only, of course. With your permission I will ride Pirate and show them all what a well-bred horse is capable of doing. I took him out on a run this morning, and I have never covered so much ground in such a short time."

As soon as he said it, he regretted it, for Willa's face fell. "I miss riding him so much," she said. "I feel that perhaps I should ask Papa to sell him so Pirate has the opportunity to run daily with his new owner, but I cannot bear to as I am already giving up so much."

John knew she spoke of her freedom of movement. "Do not," he practically demanded. "I am taking turns exercising him and my own horse. Pirate gets his daily exercise in," he assured her. Then he broached another subject. "The only thing I worry about with a house party is your safety and the safety of the other guests."

"There is safety in numbers, you know," Willa replied. "And I cannot quit living because of a few attempts to harm me. I also feel sure Mr. Parker will find out soon who the perpetrator or perpetrators most likely are."

John chose his response carefully. Willa's life had already been made so small compared to what it had been and he was finally beginning to see glimmers of her normal lightheartedness showing through when she was planning a social event. "You're right," he said at last. "You should have the house party."

"In that case," Willa announced, "we will write the invitations."

"I have the cards right here," Fayre said.

John stood up, "This is my cue to leave. I'll see you at tea time." He walked out the door and spoke quietly to Abbott, "Do you know where Mr. Parker is?"

"Mr. Parker is coming up the path at this exact moment." The butler looked out the pane of glass near the door.

John's gaze followed to see the investigator walking toward the door slowly, head down, as though deep in thought. He reached for his coat, sliding his arms into it as the butler assisted him. Buttoning the coat as he stepped toward the door, John waited as Abbott opened it and then strode out.

"Mr. Parker," he greeted the investigator. "You are just the man I wanted to see. Do you have a few minutes?"

The other man looked up, "I do indeed, my lord."

John swung into step beside him, redirecting the man to a small path leading around the side of the house. "How is the investigation going?"

"Well, my lord. I am still waiting on the reference letters to confirm my suspicions."

"And do you mind sharing those suspicions?"

"There is one person in the stables and one in the house who may be trying to kill your fiancée, my lord. What I cannot determine is why. I don't believe they are anything but hired thugs, so to speak. Perhaps once I expose them they will be willing to talk."

"Who are they are?"

"I am reluctant to say until I have confirmed my suspicions. It is too easy to ruin a person's life with unjustified rumors, my lord."

"The viscount and I ought to know, Mr. Parker. We can be trusted not to jump to a judgment."

The investigator continued walking, but finally stopped and looked up at John. "In the stables, I suspect that Jenkins has caused the accident and the other mishaps."

John thought back to the stable employees and nodded his head. "I, myself, wondered about him. How did you come to this conclusion?"

"When questioned, he did not look me in the eye. Jenkins had the means to do so and was working in the stables each time something occurred. I am anxious to know if he has worked where he stated he has."

"And in the house," John said, "who do you suspect?"

"The new nurse, Nancy," Mr. Parker stated easily enough. "She has been employed since the incidents in the house began. Again, she has the means to do so and, as a nurse, has knowledge about the amount of laudanum needed to cause Miss Dutton to be sleeping soundly when the fire began. Also, she is often in the kitchen, and the cook said the day of the poisoning, Nancy was hovering around the tea tray. It is my understanding, she has been seen talking to Jenkins on more than one occasion. In fact, the stable hands have teased Jenkins about Nancy being sweet on him."

"I cannot like her," John confided. "From the moment she arrived she has unsettled me somehow. Even my valet, Martin, has said she seems shifty eyed."

"Yes, I spoke to your man. He, after all, could not be a suspect since he was not here when the earlier incidents occurred. Martin confided in me that he suspected Nancy and how you had asked him to keep an eye on her."

The two men continued to walk side by side. "I do believe I will hear back soon on the inquiries, my lord."

❧

When it was time to prepare for dinner, Willa was carried upstairs to the Bath chair which had been returned to that level. It was nice, she mused, to have mobility on each floor. Fayre accompanied her to the second floor, but it was Molly who came outside to push the chair into the girls' bed chamber.

"Did you want to change or just freshen up, Miss Willa?" the maid asked her.

As it was quite a bit of work to change clothes, Willa had taken to only freshening up most evenings. Her family and John did not expect her to dress for dinner each night in her condition. "I'll freshen up, Molly."

Molly assisted her in washing up and was finishing doing her hair when Nancy walked in the door. "I can take Miss Willa out to be carried downstairs, Molly. That way you can help Miss Fayre with her dinner preparations."

"That's alright," Fayre said from behind the dressing screen. "I'm used to doing things myself. Molly, why don't you take Willa out?"

"I insist," Nancy said as she pushed the Bath chair toward the door of the bed chamber. Before anyone could act, Willa was being pushed rather wildly down the hallway.

"Nancy, please stop. You're frightening me," Willa commanded.

The nurse ignored her and picked up her speed. Footsteps sounded behind them, and Willa looked back to see Fayre, scantily clad in a dressing gown and Molly pounding down the hallway toward them.

"Stop this minute!" Fayre demanded.

"Nancy, please stop," Molly pleaded.

Willa realized the speed with which the nurse was pushing her was quite intentional. That was when she realized Nancy was the person who was attempting to kill her. It all fit into place. "Nancy, you are fired!" she stated emphatically.

It mattered little because Willa was given a shove toward the stairs and was soon careening down the steep stairway in a three wheeled chair. Not knowing what else to do, she screamed at the same time as did Molly and Fayre.

Chapter Fourteen

John spent an hour in the library talking to his future father-in-law about who Samuel Parker suspected as carrying out attempts on Willa's life. When the mantle clock struck six, he knew he needed to run upstairs and clean up a bit before dinner. They were keeping country hours and, even though he could get by without changing for dinner, he still did so. He made an excuse to Yale and then stood to exit the room. Just as he stepped out of the door, he heard a commotion, followed by three feminine screams. Looking up, his heart practically leapt into his throat. Willa was clinging to the Bath chair as it rushed down the stairs out of control. A look of terror was on her face, her knuckles white against the edges as she struggled to maintain her seat.

John took the stairs two at a time, grabbed the bannister, and braced himself for the impact. When it hit, the front wheel slid between his calves, and the front of the chair smashed into his lower legs, almost knocking him down. Somehow, he managed to hang on by one arm as he heard a footman and the butler dash up behind him. At the same time he became aware of Fayre swathed in a dressing gown entangled with two other women. Yes, he thought, as he watched, it was Molly and the nurse. The footman coming up the stairs grabbed the Bath chair, "Let me help, my lord."

At the same time, John was aware of a crowd of people, of two footmen pulling the young women apart at the top of the stairs, of his future in-laws, and a number of servants. Yale strode up the stairs as John and the footman held firmly onto the chair. He scooped his daughter up in his arms and as her tears started to fall, he murmured to her, "There, there, honey. It's okay. Papa's got you."

Another footman ran up the stairs to grasp the back of the chair, and with the aid of the footman next to John, lifted it and carried it back up the stairs. John could finally move. "Is she alright?" he asked of Willa.

Not giving her father a chance to reply, Willa sniffed and said, "I am. I have fired Nancy, for she shoved me down the stairs."

"Ah ha! My suspicions are correct," the investigator said as he appeared at the top of the stairs. "Is there somewhere we can detain this person until I have a chance to question her?" he asked.

It was the butler who intervened. "Yes, sir, there is a cloak closet right down here. It has a sturdy door and a lock on it and is rarely used, so it is empty. Also, it does not have a window."

Mr. Parker looked at the two footmen who now held Nancy by either arm. "Let us take her down there then. We do not need to give her a chair. She can sit on the floor. A chair would only provide her with a weapon."

John stepped aside as they moved past him on their way down and watched as the culprit was locked into the closet, the key turned by the butler and then handed to Mr. Parker who pocketed it. Yale took his daughter into the drawing room, and the viscountess hurried down to be with her. John turned to follow and realized his shins were screaming in pain. He looked down and saw blood soaking through his snug pantaloons. At the same time, Martin emerged and said, "You should come upstairs and let me tend to your wounds, my lord."

"Yes, but first I need to check on my fiancée." He continued on down the stairs and hurried into the drawing room. Inside, Blythe was sitting next to her daughter, patting and rubbing the back of her hand. Yale was looming over them both with a worried look on his face. John hurried to her side, dropped on his knees on the floor in front of her and grasped her other hand. "Are you sure you have not been hurt?"

Willa nodded. "I'm sure. I was mostly scared and mad. Oh, she has made me so angry."

"Better angry than hurt," he replied.

She searched his face, "Are you hurt, John? You must be. You threw yourself in front of me to save me."

John didn't believe in lying to her. "The chair hit my lower legs, and I believe I may have received a scratch or two, but that is all."

"You must have them tended to," she told him. "You don't want them to become infected."

"I will," he assured her, "but I needed to make sure you suffered no harm."

Blythe looked at him. "Go have them tended to, John. I have told Abbott to ask Cook to hold off on dinner for a while. That will give us all time to settle a bit."

John rose, wincing as he did so. "I won't be long," he promised.

Upstairs, Martin glanced at John's buff breeches. "If we get those off right away, I should be able to soak the bloodstains out of them," his trusted valet said. John sat down and let the other man assist with pulling his boots off, followed by his pants. As Martin carefully peeled them away from his bloody shins, John winced once again. Then he sat there as his servant tended to his wounds. The skin was broken on both legs where the runaway chair had crashed into him. "You'll have some quite colorful bruises in a day or two, my lord," Martin remarked.

"Yes, I expect I will," John agreed. "I suspect they'll be feeling quite stiff tomorrow, as well."

A half hour later, John's wounds were bandaged and he was dressed for dinner. He made his way downstairs where he joined the Dutton family for an aperitif they doubtlessly all needed. "Do you know if Mr. Parker has questioned Nancy yet?" he quietly asked Yale as he stood next to the viscount near the window.

"He is in with her now, I believe." In fact, at that moment the man emerged from the cloak closet and walked toward them.

Yale turned to him, "Mr. Parker, we are glad to see you. How has your questioning gone?"

"Not well. She is refusing to talk other than to say it was an accident, that she tripped and the chair escaped her grasp. Of course, I do not believe her. However, I am confident she is not behind this, that she is only hired. After all, the risk she took was too great if she were not receiving a substantial payment. Yet I cannot get her to admit anything."

"The attempts may not stop if we do not find out who the culprit is," John said.

"That is true, no doubt," the investigator stated. "I will be taking her to London tomorrow to face multiple counts of attempted murder. The closet seems to be secure, so if we could perhaps provide her with a pallet and a chamber pot, along with a plate of dinner, she might be more willing to talk in the morn. Do you think we could round up enough men to guard the door throughout the night?"

"By all means," the viscount replied.

❦

The household seemed to settle a bit with the knowledge Nancy had been taken to prison in London to await trial. Even though the nurse had tried to kill her at least three times, Willa was soft hearted enough to hope she did not hang. Transportation to Australia was another thing – knowing the woman was on the other side of the earth would make Willa much more comfortable.

As it turned out, Nancy had been no more willing to talk the following morning. Instead, she had been led off in handcuffs by Samuel Parker. The morning brought the additional news that Jenkins, the groom who had been suspected of the other attempts on Willa's life, had disappeared in the night. While this didn't leave Willa completely safe and secure, knowing he was not on the property did help.

With the feeling of having to constantly watch over her shoulder gone, Willa turned to the final details of her house party. The invitations had been sent, and responses were beginning to trickle in. So far, everyone had accepted her invitation, and the replies were both thankful and enthusiastic. Indeed, entertainments could be somewhat thin at this time of the year.

Willa did not move back into her own room. When it became known a day after the last attempt on Willa's life that both Jenkins and Nancy had falsified their references, Willa felt it wiser not to let her parents replace the nurse. Dawson had adjusted both Bath chairs and was working on a lifting device for her, leaving Willa feeling she was much more independent than she had been. With Brooks and Fayre accompanying her, she had even taken the pony cart out to deliver invitations to the neighbors for her events. Fayre walked them to the doors, but Willa drove as close to the door as she could each time.

She spent many hours with John and had begun to drop hints that she intended to release him.

"Fayre and I drove to Townsend Park Farms to deliver an invitation for several events to Miss Marty," she told him.

"Did you?" he replied almost absently as he pushed her chair toward the stables to visit Pirate.

"She seemed quite excited to be joining us for so many events. In fact, she said she was glad that farming doesn't require much of her time during this season. I think she works too hard, don't you?"

"It's her choice, Willa," was his reply. "I suspect the farm provides well enough she could hire a farm manager if she so chose."

Another time she brought up her other expected female guests. "I'm sure Miss Russell would love to meet her match at my party. Why, she will make a wonderful wife. She is gracious and intelligent."

"Not many men are worried about whether their prospective wives are intelligent, Willa dear," he had said.

"You are."

"Indeed I am, but I am rare. Besides, I already have a prospective wife. One whom I hope will decide she can go ahead and marry me right away."

"But what if whoever hired Jenkins and Nancy hires someone else who is more successful this time? Then you would need another prospective wife."

"Don't even joke about that, Willa. I love you and would grieve for the rest of my life and never marry anyone else."

"But you need an heir."

"I have an heir," he said, "albeit he is one and twenty, still has spots, and knows nothing about agriculture. Still, he is no doubt holding his breath, hoping I will expire without a son in my future."

Another time she said, "Miss Clarke will make the most exceptional mother," Willa said. "I can see her with herds of little children hiding behind her skirts."

"Hmm, I hope our children will have enough confidence not to hide behind your skirts."

"Don't be silly, John. They wouldn't be able to hide behind my skirts as all I can do is sit down."

"It is irrelevant, Willa. Our children will be more likely to want to ride on your lap, yelling, 'Faster Mama, faster!'"

Two days later she brought Miss Matthews into the conversation. "I have heard Miss Matthews is a lover of animals," she ventured.

"No doubt she has a yappy little dog she takes everywhere."

Honestly, Willa thought he sounded grumpy. "What is wrong with a little dog? You have dogs."

"Yes, I do. Working dogs. They earn their keep working with animals or hunting. They do not sit around on a cushion all day doing nothing more than leaving hair behind and panting."

Willa gave up. It was not easy to bring up the topic she needed to bring up. She would just have to show John he would be better off without her.

The first day of her house party arrived at last. John's friends, the married Earl and Countess of Tabor, were the first to drive down the road toward the estate. Willa saw them from the drawing room door and, although it probably wasn't keeping with propriety, she wheeled herself out to the door where Abbott obligingly opened it and helped her across the threshold so she greeted her first guests on the front step. She noticed John walking toward her from the stables, arriving before the carriage came to a halt. As his friends stepped out of the vehicle, John walked down to greet them.

"Tabor," he greeted, "it is good to see you. And, of course, Melinda, it is even better to see you," he joked.

The two men fell into conversation almost immediately, and the young countess made her own way up to the door where she greeted Willa.

"Miss Dutton, thank you for inviting us. I am so looking forward to this party."

"As am I," Willa replied, "but please call me Willa. I am hoping we will soon be fast friends."

"I am sure we will be. Why, you are to marry one of my husband's good friends, and we will no doubt see each other often."

Willa did not comment but instead invited her guest in for a refreshing cup of tea. They had barely settled by the tea service, when Miss Caroline Russell and her parents arrived. After that, everyone seemed to arrive quite quickly. The maids were busy carrying in tray after tray laden with fresh tea, plates of delicate sandwiches, and a variety of delicious biscuits and cakes. Meanwhile, the footmen hauled in trunks of clothing and possessions, while Mrs. Bailey was kept busy directing valets and maidservants to their employers' rooms.

As it was well into the fall, Willa had chosen a pretty, golden apricot gown for the evening. It was a new gown, purchased from the seamstress in the village who was more than pleased to have the opportunity to impress the titled with her skills, for she had fantasies of moving to London. When Willa had explained she had a need to freely move her arms while wheeling her chair, the woman had suggested that instead of following the style of long, fitted sleeves, she create full sleeves with tight, deep cuffs. The neckline was quite low, allowing her mother's borrowed pearls to be displayed to their best. Willa felt quite beautiful in the gown despite having to be in her chair.

With just over two dozen dinner guests squeezed in around the dining table, the quarters were close. Even though Willa's chair fit under the table now, she had asked to be lifted into a dining chair to save space. Seated someway down the table, between Baron Macey and Mr. Webster, Willa experienced a certain amount of pride as dish after dish was exclaimed over. Certainly, Cook and her staff had prepared the food, but it had been herself and Fayre who had toiled over the menu. Conversation flowed freely as the houseguests made themselves known to those from the neighborhood. As the final course drew to a close, Willa asked Morton to lift her into the waiting chair and wheel her into the drawing room.

When the gentlemen joined the ladies after their brandies and cigars, Willa suggested those with musical talents perform on the pianoforte for the benefit of the others. She recommended Fayre begin and, reminiscent of the earlier dinner party she had held, young Ronald Hampstead was happy to turn pages for her cousin. When Fayre had played several numbers, Willa coaxed each of her younger eligible female guests to play. The gentlemen, of course, were willing to turn pages, sing along, and generally flirt with the women.

Willa kept an eye on John. As might be expected, he spent a considerable amount of time with his closest friend, the Earl of Tabor. However, as John was well bred, he did not restrict his time to just one person. Instead, he made his way around the room.

Indeed, John did know that as Willa was the hostess, he more or less played the role of host, although the party wasn't in his own home. He would have liked to spend all of his time with Tabor, but he did not. He spoke to Baron Macey about the viscount's horses, to the Earl of Baddock about the hunting available in the area. He pointed out to Mr. Donald Miller when the elder Miss Matthews was alone for a moment, knowing the man needed a mother for all of those children. John greeted the married women and complimented each of the single ones on their pianoforte performances. At last, he worked his way around to Miss Marty Robinson.

"Willa and I are pleased you could take time away from your livestock to join us for the festivities," he remarked.

"It is my pleasure. I will admit life is a bit dull at the farm these days."

"It's not calving season," John pointed out.

"No, and I sold my wandering bull to a Scotsman who has had his eye on my herd for a while now. The man has a large amount of land in the wilds of Scotland, and I'm sure my bull is happier there than being restricted to a small pen to keep him home."

"No doubt," John agreed. "I do hope you received a good price for him."

He watched as the woman smiled, noting how much her face lit up when she did so. "I did. After all, the bull has proven himself time and time again. With my cows, with the herd to the north, the one to the south, and with the ones in both the east and west."

John laughed outright. "Proliferate fellow, isn't he?" He paused, looking around to see if he dare spend some more time with this woman. Noting that everyone was occupied, he continued. "When do you start calving season?"

"In March. I am not complaining about it being slow now, mind you. I keep calving season as short and compacted as I possibly can. At that time, I make sure I have a man scheduled 'round the clock so I do not have any losses. Of course, right after that we must keep an eye on all those delightful mamas and babies so none of them fall ill."

John was well aware of the work involved in farming, especially when one had a reputation like Marty Robinson's. He spent the next quarter hour in conversation with her, enjoying every last minute. Finally and regretfully, he excused himself to move on, but only when Viscount Gage joined them and he could be sure Miss Marty would not stand alone. He was unsure if she had much in common with most of the women in attendance.

※

Willa watched John with Miss Marty. Willa was speaking to Miss Clarke and her new friend, Melinda. It was a struggle to keep an eye on her fiancé while still carrying on a sensible conversation with the other two.

She had seen him walk up to Miss Marty. Before that time he had been doing a remarkable job of playing host to her hostess role. Once he had joined the other woman, however, he had loitered. Due to the size of the room, she wasn't close enough to hear what they were conversing about. However, she did note Miss Marty's face had broken into a lovely smile which lit up her entire countenance. Later, John's burst of laughter had been easy to catch. This had been accompanied by his own smile, the one he formed when he was truly enjoying himself.

Willa almost sighed in satisfaction. While it made her heart ache yet again to think of giving him up, she knew it was for the best. And knowing the man she loved with her whole being was settled with a woman with whom he had much in common, who could provide him with healthy and rambunctious heirs, and who would make him laugh and smile was all that mattered to her now.

Chapter Fifteen

For the next day, Willa and her cousin had planned a tour of the gardens for the ladies, while the viscount and John took the gentlemen on a tour of the stables. While Willa was capable of pushing her own chair now, she wasn't yet in the condition for pushing it long distances or over rough ground. Consequently, her favorite footman, Morton, accompanied the women through the grounds, pushing Willa's chair. The weather was pleasant without anything more than the gentlest of breezes, and they all enjoyed seeing the autumn plants. Willa noted that her mother seemed to be enjoying herself and realized suddenly that she had been staying at home much more than normal since the accident. It saddened her to realize how much she had inadvertently effected everyone's life.

It was in the afternoon, when they organized an archery tournament. Chairs were assembled on one of the patios for the older attendees, while the younger guests practiced archery. Due to the differences in skill levels between the genders, Fayre recommended that each gentleman choose the name of a lady to be on his team. The scores, then, would be for the two of them. As she passed around the hat with the young women's names in them, Willa watched anxiously to see whose name John drew. He looked at her, winked, and said, "I drew my fiancée's name."

No, that would not do. He must draw one of the other women's names. Calmly, Willa spoke aloud. "Well then, John, to be sporting, you must put it back and draw another. After all, Tabor did not select his own wife's."

Willa received help from an unlikely source. Mr. William Webster chimed in, "Yes, Roydon, you must draw again. I have been watching Miss Dutton and made note of how skilled she is at pushing her own chair around. She is by far the strongest of the women here, and some of us need that benefit far more than you do."

"Indeed, Roydon, I am flabby compared to you, and I had hoped to draw Miss Dutton's name for myself," Viscount Gage spoke.

John could do nothing else than to put Willa's name back in the hat and draw out a second choice. He smiled at his second draw. "Lady Tabor!" He strolled over to his friend's wife and held out his arm. "Melinda, shall we show this pitiful group of archers just how it is done?"

Willa fumed silently. This was not helping her plan. However, she moved ahead with the activity, having had her name drawn by Mr. Hart. She had not practiced archery in some time, certainly not since before the accident, but she found that she shot the arrow with more force than before. The chair caused her to be shorter, and so she had to aim up, but it did not seem to make any difference, for she and Mr. Hart easily won the tournament.

That evening when playing cards, Willa waited as the guests seated themselves. While she was needed to make an even number of tables, she pretended she had to see Abbott about something. This way she was delayed, and by the time she was ready to wheel herself to a table, Miss Russell and the Earl of Shelton had already made up the table with John. Even though John would be her partner, she could use the time to promote Miss Russell to him.

Miss Russell had not taken during season after season. In fact, Willa had just learned that Miss Russell was four and twenty. It was not that she was unattractive, although she did need a dresser who would assist her in selecting more complimentary colors to go with her dark blonde hair and lackluster gray eyes. It was that Miss Russell was a bit of a bluestocking. This aspect of her personality, however, was what had prompted Willa to invite her. John appreciated a clever mind and a quick wit. She decided to use the opportunity to make John more aware of both Miss Russell and Miss Marty all at the same time.

"Did I hear, Miss Russell, that you started a book club in London?" Willa said.

"Yes." The woman was obviously proud of her group, as the smile she offered carried into her gray eyes and they changed from lackluster to enlivened. "We are a select group of ladies who read books chosen for enlightenment or the improvement of the mind."

Willa noticed John seemed interested. "Do you read an assigned portion of the book, then, much like we did at university?" he asked.

Miss Russell said drolly, "Since women are not allowed to attend university, I cannot say for sure. However, we do choose what amount we can read each week. For example, last week we chose to read three chapters."

"Then you discuss it?" Willa prompted.

"As we read, we each write down one discussion question per chapter, and then at our meetings we spend our time in conversation over those." She laughed heartily. "It can become quite interesting. Not everyone agrees with the rest of the group, and we have had some lively arguments."

"I remember those at school," John pointed out. "I always enjoyed the arguments, didn't you, Shelton?"

The other man said, "Honestly, I didn't enjoy the arguments much. In fact, I usually looked out the window wishing everyone would be silent and let us move on with our studies so we might be dismissed early. I much preferred spending my time in the boxing ring or fencing with a worthy opponent."

"Well, I always enjoyed the argument," John returned. "In fact, I often started the argument despite what side I was on."

Miss Russell sat up straighter. "I do that in my book club," she said. "I often agree with what the others are saying, but I enjoy the discussion so much I occasionally choose to play the devil's advocate."

The conversation at the table grew livelier with that statement. John and Miss Russell seemed to be quite attuned to each other's methods of discussion. It was so much so, that Willa began to feel sorry for the other earl and finally steered the conversation around a bit to better include him by saying, "I must agree with the earl. I used to hope my governess would dismiss me early so I might escape to the stables."

The next day brought a scavenger hunt in the afternoon. As hostess, Willa was forced to bow out of the activity since she had designed the game, as had her cousin. The older guests did not participate while the younger guests were divided into teams of three each. Willa put her fiancé with Miss Clark and the Earl of Tabor. A married man would offer him no competition for the younger woman. Miss Matthews had been teamed with the earl's wife and Mr. Hart. That left Miss Russell with Mr. Webster and the young viscount. Mr. Miller and the older Miss Matthews had been drafted to participate on Lord Shelton's team. The re quirements took them over much of the estate. They had clues leading them to the stables, to the attics, throughout other areas of the house, and even into the village. Willa had made sure four buggies were ready at the front door when each team needed them. She and Fayre spent the time they were all occupied to check over their plans for the remainder of the party.

John's group was the second to return, joining Mr. Hart's group in the drawing room for tea. As they entered, John was laughing, his familiar face wreathed in a smile and his blue eyes dancing with excitement. The others, too, seemed merry and

Willa was sure Miss Clark had seized the opportunity to let John get acquainted with her rather delightful personality.

Willa had invited Miss Marty and the young Mr. Hampstead to participate in an excursion in mid-week. The younger set piled into open vehicles in groups of four. Willa insisted on the pony trap being readied for herself. It was lower and easier for her to be lifted into, and since they had two more than would fit in the other vehicles, it made sense. Intending to take Fayre with her, Willa was surprised when John leapt in beside her and reached for the reins. "I intended to take Fayre with me," she announced somewhat coolly. John leaned toward her, his upper body brushing hers, "I told her to ride with Ronald Hampstead. They are of an age and are both a little out of place with the rest of us being somewhat older. I put them in with Tabor and Melinda, so they are well chaperoned and cared for. Besides, I have not been allowed to spend enough time with you."

Willa said little in reply. After all, she could hardly say, "But you are to spend time with Miss Clark, Miss Matthews, Miss Russell, or Miss Marty. You must find another woman to marry!" Instead, she remained quiet and let her love take over the control of the horse pulling the trap.

As John led the way down the lane toward the ruins, he said, "Your party is a success."

"I do hope so. Everyone seems to be enjoying themselves, but I still worry."

"The scavenger hunt yesterday was a smashing success," he said. "I know for a fact everyone had a good time."

"Yes, you and your party seemed to have fun. Certainly, you were all laughing when you arrived."

"Miss Clark has a wonderful sense of humor. She has a way of regaling stories to ensure everyone laughs."

"Oh, she does, doesn't she? She must keep those close to her smiling all the time."

The weather the next day was perfect for Willa's plans, and the entire party walked to a nearby lake where they were met by footmen who had fishing paraphernalia and a picnic lunch set up. Willa drove herself there in the pony cart, accompanied only by Brooks. She insisted everyone else should walk to enjoy the unseasonably warm weather and the exercise. Willa did not fish when she arrived, as it was difficult to get close enough to the shore in her Bath chair; however, she enjoyed watching the others. It was Miss Matthews who approached John and asked for some coaching on casting techniques. Willa watched with interest, but noted her fiancé was never less than circumspect.

The neighbors joined them that evening, and Cook treated them all to trout almandine made from the bounty caught that day. After dinner, Willa organized charades. She knew for a fact Vicar Wright particularly enjoyed them, and she counted on him to keep the excitement for them moving along. At one point in the game, Miss Marty was acting out a book title. Most of the group seemed clueless as to what she was attempting to portray when suddenly John burst out with the title. "You seem to be sympathetic with Miss Marty," Willa commented to him quietly as he was sitting next to her.

"I would have acted it out exactly the same way," he replied.

That night, in the room she still shared with Fayre, Willa mused about the progress of her goal of letting John go. He seemed to enjoy all the women she had invited. She still felt, however, that Miss Marty had more in common with John, and tonight had been an example of how compatible they were. The next day, she had scheduled a horse race and invited all the neighbors in for the day. She would need to corner Miss Marty again to get her reaction over John. Willa sighed, suddenly wishing with all of her heart that she could roll over.

"What are you thinking?" came Fayre's voice through the dark.

"A lot of things, but primarily I wish I could roll over."

Fayre threw the covers back. "Why didn't you just ask me? I'm perfectly capable of helping you roll over." She walked around the bed and pulled Willa's covers down to the bottom of the bed. "Toward the middle of the bed?"

"Yes, please."

"Twist your torso that way and I'll move your hips and legs."

The two worked together and finally, with a huge sigh, Willa lay on her side. Fayre covered her back up and hurried around the bed to crawl in beside her, facing the center as well. "Now you can tell me what else is on your mind," she said to Willa.

"It's complicated," Willa hedged.

"You know, I am pretty intelligent. I'm almost eighteen and I have been educated by my parents. My father especially has had me read all types of treatises and lectures and sermons. I can understand complicated."

"Of course you can," Willa said apologetically. "It's, well...it's personal."

"I'm a vicar's daughter. I have also learned how to be discreet. You wouldn't believe what I have overheard parishioners telling my father, yet no one has any idea I know. My father and mother have also taught me to be wise."

Willa finally chuckled. "You're right. You are all of those things – smart, educated, discreet, and wise. And it would feel good to talk to someone."

Fayre lay patiently on her side of the bed, waiting for Willa to begin. At last, she did. "I have decided to release John from our engagement."

That got her cousin's attention. She sat straight up in bed with an exclaimed, "No!"

"Yes," Willa replied calmly.

"I thought you loved him." Fayre sounded almost hurt that she might have believed something of Willa that was not true.

"I do love him," Willa whispered. "That's why I've decided to let him go."

"I don't understand."

Willa searched for the words to explain herself and finally, remembering their first trip to Townsend Park Farms in the pony trap, she peered at Fayre through the darkness. "Do you remember when we first took the pony trap over to Townsend Park Farms?"

"Of course," came the reply.

"Do you remember how Miss Marty was looking at the bull, the one behind the extra high fence?"

"Yes, she said she had to have the fence increased in height because he always jumped the other fences."

"And she was thinking of selling him," Willa reminded Fayre. "She told us he was her favorite bull, but she knew he couldn't be happy when she had to lock him up to keep him home."

"I remember," Fayre said as she snuggled back down into the bed.

"The other night I heard Miss Marty tell John she had sold the bull to a man in Scotland. Someone who has a lot of land so the bull would have more room to be free. That is why I am going to let John go."

Fayre was silent for a bit. "I guess I am not as intelligent and wise as I thought because I don't understand, Willa."

"I'm paralyzed, Fayre. I can no longer walk, or ride, or dance. John and I have always loved to ride together, whether it is sedately through a park or headlong over the open land. Now I can't."

"I don't think your relationship is built only on the fact you can ride together," her cousin suggested kindly.

"No, it isn't," Willa said patiently, "but it's not just that. Both Dr. Saunders and Dr. Lead warned me about having children. Dr. Saunders has said I don't dare risk it. I prefer to think Dr. Lead might know more and he said I can have them, but I shouldn't rush into it in case it might make my condition worse. John deserves an heir. Indeed, he needs an heir, Fayre. It is his duty."

The two were silent for a while, each lost in their own thoughts. Finally, Willa continued. "That is why I am having the party. I want him to meet other eligible women, to realize he needs to let me go because I am afraid, otherwise, when I tell him, he will do the honorable thing and refuse."

"He would," Fayre agreed. "Your John is an honorable man."

"I have been watching them. Miss Russell is a bluestocking, and I think John admires her. They both like to start arguments in a discussion just for the sake of starting them."

Fayre laughed lightly. "I can see that of both of them."

"And he said he admires Miss Clark's sense of humor. When they came back from the scavenger hunt, they were all laughing. I remarked on it and he told me she had a wonderful sense of humor."

"I'm not sure it means anything, Willa. Most everyone likes a person with a wonderful sense of humor unless they are exceptionally dour."

"This is true," Willa admitted, "but there might have been something more there. It is difficult to tell. And, you were busy visiting with Ronald Hampstead, but I noticed Miss Matthews approached John today at the lake. She asked him to demonstrate casting techniques to her."

"I did notice, Willa, and it is not like he wrapped his arms around her or anything. I don't think you can assume anything from the incident."

"Perhaps not," Willa agreed reluctantly, "but I know he admires Miss Marty. Tonight, when he guessed the book title she was portraying that no one else could, he told me he would have acted it out in the exact same way."

Fayre remained quiet.

"And they share so much interest in agriculture and livestock. Have you heard them talk about their cattle?"

"I can't say I have," Fayre said.

"They both enjoy the conversation immensely. You can hear it in the tone of their voices and see it in their faces. They are like, well, quite good friends. Don't you see? They would be perfect for each other. They have many shared interests, and Miss Marty could provide him with healthy babies, and she could ride with him. In fact, she would probably ride astride!"

"So your plan is to tell John you do not want to marry him and then encourage him to court Miss Marty instead?"

"Exactly."

Chapter Sixteen

The house party was over, and the guests were beginning to leave. John was ready for them all to be gone. Something had been going on with Willa, and he was determined to get to the root of it. She had insisted he spend time with the other guests, something he would have done naturally. But it seemed to him like she was intentionally pushing the single females toward him. He had been forced to spend extra time with Miss Matthews, Miss Russell, and Miss Clark. Then, when the neighbors had joined them, Willa had made sure he spent plenty of time with Miss Marty Robinson. This seemed unusual to him as most young women preferred their fiancés did not spend time with other eligible women. Additionally, there had been a few times when she seemed cool toward him, even irritated that he wanted to spend time with her. It was almost as if she was pushing him away.

When the last guest had left, he turned to find her and saw she was being carried up the stairs by Morton. He bounded up after them. "Willa, I would like to speak with you privately."

"John, I'm exhausted after all the activities. I am going to spend the afternoon relaxing and napping. Another time, perhaps."

He had been dismissed. Thoroughly dismissed. Feeling completely rejected he strolled to the stables to exercise one of the horses. Even a long, fast ride on Pirate did little to blow away the emotions he was experiencing.

John made it through the evening, in which every time he tried to speak to Willa she brushed him off. Finally, she claimed a headache and went to bed early. The next morning, she sent down word with Molly that she was feeling poorly – her headache was lingering – and she would relax in a darkened room before having a light lunch served to her there. Once again, John was left cooling his heels. He spent the morning dealing with business from afar by writing to his steward in response to the man's last letter. He also wrote to his mother, updating her on the status of Willa's condition and trying to amuse her with tales of the house party. That afternoon he took his own horse out for a ride, going into the village for lack of a better destination.

As he passed the church, John decided to stop to see if the vicar was in. Tying up his horse, he opened the door and stepped into the darkened interior of the church. The vicar was indeed in, for he was practicing his sermon behind the pulpit. Upon seeing his visitor, the man stopped in mid-sentence. "Lord Roydon," he said in a friendly tone.

John walked further in. "Vicar," he greeted. "I hope I am not intruding."

The man stepped down from the altar. "You are not. I was only practicing my sermon, and, frankly, any interruption is welcome. Some weeks I feel my sermon lacks something, perhaps verve, and this is one of those weeks." He shook John's hand. "What brings you by on this fine autumn day?"

"Oh, I was just out exercising my horse and thought I would stop by."

"Life at the estate must be dull today after the activities of the past sennight."

"I would not say it is dull. Actually, I welcome a return to the normalcy we have developed."

"I can understand that, although my wife and I heartily enjoyed joining the festivities upon occasion. The village social life can seem lacking at times, and it is always nice to have a break from the routine."

John looked around, noticing the artistic stained glass window above the altar. At last, he looked at the vicar. "I am worried about my fiancée and cannot talk to her family about it. I thought perhaps you wouldn't mind listening and offering any advice you might have."

"Of course. Why don't we have a seat?" The man indicated a close pew and John sat down, leaving room for the vicar to sit near him. "Tell me; what's on your mind, my lord."

John thought before he spoke and finally said, "Her behavior toward me has changed. She seems cooler, and I do believe she is avoiding me." The vicar remained silent beside him, so John went on. "Perhaps I am imagining things, but I feel as if she was trying to push the other single women at me during the party. It's almost like she was trying to get me to swing my attentions from her to one of the others." He let the silence stretch for a bit and then went on. "I am wondering if she no longer loves me, or if she ever did love me, but when I try to talk to her she avoids me and puts me off."

The vicar spoke up rather quickly. "I am sure she loves you, my lord. Positive of it, in fact." And here he was quiet for a bit as though he was selecting his words carefully. "Sometimes, however, a person acts in this way out of love. I think you must try to talk to her, get her to open up to you."

Having nothing else to say, John rose, and the vicar followed suit. The older man turned to him and said, "I cannot break the confidence of a parishioner, my lord, but I feel strongly that Miss Willa has something she wants to tell you, but she may be struggling with how to say it, as well as with what your reaction will be. Trust me, you must open up a conversation with her."

With those vague but sage words ringing in his ears, John left the church. He collected his horse and walked him through the village until he arrived at the few shops that lined the main road. Here he once again tied up his horse and then walked into the shop where he had purchased the pretty fan for Willa hoping to find some trinket she might enjoy.

He had made the trip around the store's small interior before he noticed it. There, on a hook in a dim corner, was a dark brown bonnet trimmed with feathers in a variety of tans and rich browns. A bright orange ribbon encircled it and ended in a jaunty bow in the back. He loitered, imagining it on her as she rode in the pony trap down a country road.

"May I help you, my lord?" the shopkeeper spoke. Everyone in the village knew who he was, he had been there so long.

"Yes, I would like to see that bonnet," he pointed toward it. "The brown felt one," he added for clarification.

The shopkeeper took it down. "It would be lovely on Miss Dutton," the woman said. "Most women pass it by as they don't believe it to be feminine enough, but Miss Dutton is a young lady much at home with nature."

"Was it made locally?" he asked.

"Indeed, it was. My eldest daughter trimmed it."

John picked up the hat and turned it around and around. "She is quite talented. I do believe I will purchase it."

"If it is not too forward of me to ask, how is she, our Miss Dutton?"

"She is adjusting," John answered. "There has been no improvement in her condition, but we are all trying to find ways for her to be more mobile and to learn to live in her new life."

The woman tut-tutted. "So sad. It is just so sad."

When John walked into the house, he inquired as to whether Miss Willa was up. "No, my lord," Abbott said. "Miss Fayre is in the parlour, however."

John handed him the hat box. Could you have this placed in my bed chamber?"

"Certainly, my lord."

John removed his coat with the butler's assistance and then went into the parlour, where Fayre was sitting quietly, her feet tucked under her, reading a book.

"Good afternoon," he said to his fiancée's cousin.

She looked up at him and smiled, "Hello, John. You smell like the outdoors."

John seated himself. "Since I have been out riding that seems logical."

"Did you ride somewhere fun?"

"I went into the village. The vicar was practicing his sermon, so I talked to him for a bit and then went into the shops and bought a gift for Willa. He reached into his jacket pocket and pulled out the small box of sweets he had purchased for Fayre. "I got these for you."

Her young face burst into a wide smile. "Sweets! I do so love sweets." She reached for the box and quickly opened it, starting to select one and then thinking better of it. "Would you like one?" she asked, proffering the box.

"Thank you, but no," he replied. "I haven't much of a sweet tooth."

He watched as she popped one into her mouth. "Thank you. I do so appreciate it."

John was silent for a few moments, wondering whether or not to put her in the middle of his troubles with Willa. It might not be fair he thought, but he was desperate, and he had to turn to someone. "Do you think Willa will see me today?" he asked her.

Fayre hesitated before answering, "I don't know. She claims to feel bad, but ..." She looked down as she trailed off.

"But?" John prompted.

"I went up to check on her, and she is sitting in her Bath chair near the window and reading. Usually, when I have a headache I don't like to read. I just sit quietly with my eyes closed until it goes away."

John got up and walked to the window. "I feel she is avoiding me."

Fayre did not reply. In fact, when he turned back she was studying her hands.

He walked back, sat, and leaned forward in his chair. "You know something don't you?"

Her voice quivered a bit when she answered. "I told her I could be discreet."

"We all know you can," he replied, "but should you be? If it can benefit someone, perhaps being discreet is not the best option." He fell quiet, giving Fayre time to think about what he had said.

Finally, she burst forth worriedly. "She wants to release you from your engagement."

"What?" Having not meant to raise his voice, John took a calming breath and then apologized. "I'm sorry, Fayre. You surprised me, and I let myself express that a little too much. Tell me what you mean."

"She thinks you should marry someone else. Someone who can walk and dance and ride. Willa is worried she won't be able to provide you with an heir." The young woman looked up at him imploringly. "She loves you enough to release you."

It all fell into place. John realized why she had pushed him toward the other women, for that matter possibly even why she had hosted the house party. He shoved his hands through his hair and then stood up to pace once again. "How can she think I could ever marry anyone else? I love her."

"She thinks you could eventually love someone else. I believe she has Miss Marty in mind for you."

"Because I enjoy talking about cattle to her? I like her, but as a friend. I could never love her or marry her." He paced a bit more. "I still don't understand why Willa would think I wouldn't want to marry her just because she is paralyzed."

"We went to see Miss Marty," Fayre said. "I believe you had been there before us and Willa perhaps thought you cared for Miss Marty more than you did for her."

"What utter nonsense," he burst in.

Fayre waited patiently. "Miss Marty had a bull which kept jumping fences until she built the fence extra high and restricted him to only a small space."

John stopped and stared at her. "Yes, she told me. She said the other night that she sold him to a man in Scotland."

"That's right," Fayre replied. "When we were there, she told us she was thinking of selling him. That he was her favorite bull, but he was unhappy being restricted and she cared for him enough to let him go."

John said, "This is ridiculous," and he strode out of the room. Thinking better of it, he turned around and stuck his head back into the room. "Thank you, Fayre. I promise we will name our first born after you."

Fayre giggled. "What if it is a boy?"

"I'll teach him to be tough," were his parting words as he hurried toward the stairway and up to the second floor. He paused long enough to knock, but when he heard the quiet, "I'm resting," he turned the knob and made his way into the room. Indeed, Willa was sitting in her Bath chair at an angle near the window. A book lay open in her lap. She looked unbearably sad. He would wager she hadn't turned a page in a long while.

"I've asked to be left alone, John. Please honor my request."

John walked across the room and fell to his knees in front of her. He removed the book from her lap and placed it out of her reach should she decide to throw it at him. Then he picked up both of her hands, encasing them in his own. "Willa, sweetheart, we need to talk."

"Yes, we do," she agreed. Before she could get any more words out, however, he went on.

"It's time we marry. We have postponed it long enough."

"No, I refuse to marry you, John. In fact, I am releasing you from our engagement so you can marry someone else, someone whole. I believe you should court Miss Marty. You have much in common."

"Absolutely not," he declared emphatically. "If I do not marry you, I will marry no one. I love you, Willa. I love you more than riding horses, more than dancing, more than having children. I love you and I want to spend the rest of my life with you."

"But I am paralyzed and cannot be a proper wife to you."

"Because you cannot move your legs, you cannot love me?"

"That's not it," she said.

"That is the only expectation I have of a proper wife, Willa. I want you to love me." He reached up and gently grasped her chin in one hand forcing her to look him in the eyes. "Do you love me, Willa?"

She looked away and then straight back at him. "Of course, I love you, John. I love you enough to release you."

He didn't reply. Instead, he rose up on his knees, released her hands and leaned ahead. He captured her lips with his and caressed them ever so gently at first, but with increasing urgency as the kiss progressed. At last he lifted his head and murmured, "I don't want to be released, my love. You have well and truly captured my heart and it will never be set free again. I am not like Miss Marty's bull which you and Fayre met. You see, I don't need to be released because I do not want to jump fences. I am not looking for greener pastures. My pasture is already paradise."

"Hear, hear," came from the open doorway. "I think, my dear, we need to get back to planning the wedding," the viscount said to his wife.

John and Willa looked over to find Fayre, along with her aunt and uncle crowded into the doorway of the room. John rose to his feet. "Yes, I believe Noel and Claire should return from their travels soon. I see no reason why our wedding needs to be postponed at all. Let us return to our original date, a fortnight hence."

❧

The days ahead sped by for Willa. She half-heartedly suggested to John a few more times that he should let her release him. However, each time she did, he kissed her to silence her. He no longer cared who saw, and so Willa began to torment him on purpose.

"Are you sure you wouldn't prefer to marry Miss Clarke? You said yourself she has a great sense of hum..." She was silenced by a kiss. This in the parlor in the midst of tea.

"I think you should consider marrying Miss Marty," she said one day at the stables while feeding Pirate an apple over the stall gate. "She so loves..." At least three stable employees witnessed the earl giving her a rather lusty kiss to silence her. Young Jem, the tack boy, had the audacity to applaud, while both Brooks and Ward were caught chuckling at the scene before them.

"Miss Russell could no doubt quote you the science behind a kiss and even discuss with you the most famous literary lovers..." That kiss happened in private, in the West Garden, so it lasted quite a bit longer than the others.

As the wedding plans had been halted and then renewed, it was decided they would downsize them a bit. They would be married in the local church by Vicar Wright and Willa's uncle. Her uncle was ecstatic to be asked to perform the ceremony. The Duke of Lamberton would return in time to stand up with John, and the new duchess would serve as the bride's attendant. Fayre was frantically practicing the pianoforte, for she was to provide the music. Her parents and sisters were to arrive in plenty of time to celebrate the marriage with their family.

The local seamstress had been retained to create a wedding dress. Her previous design of looser sleeves so she could wheel her chair had worked so well, Willa insisted on a similar design. Willa's father, however, would push the chair down the aisle in the small church but at the wedding breakfast at the estate Willa would not be reliant on others if she wanted to move for a short distance. The seamstress had been willing to drive out to the Amhearst estate with some samples of fabric and Willa, with the aid of her mother and Fayre, selected a wonderful rich ivory brocade. It became known far and wide that the dressmaker was too busy creating a dream wedding gown for the future Countess of

Roydon, to be bothered with any other orders. Indeed, the small seed pearls, alone, would take hours of stitching.

The current Countess of Roydon arrived several days before the wedding. Her carriage was laden down with luggage, and her entourage included her maid, her companion, and her newly acquired lapdog. She announced to all and sundry that the tiny canine was necessary to keep her company in the dower house, a home not far from the main house to which she had already moved. Lady Roydon told her son she would be quite comfortable in her new home. "In truth," she told him, "I should have moved there a long time ago. It is much less house and is warmer and far more comfortable, although I do feel the gardens need some work come spring."

"I will send my gardeners over at the first sign of the season," he promised.

Willa had made the decision to restrict the invitations to the locals and family members. It was rumored that the neighboring women, including Miss Marty, had had to travel to the next village over to find a seamstress with enough free time to clothe them for the event of the year. Cook had approached Abbott about hiring some temporary assistance in the kitchen. "There's many local women who could use the extra money," she had said, "and I cannot be expected to produce a wedding breakfast to be remembered for years to come without the assistance."

The butler, then, had approached Lady Amhearst and had been assured he had carte blanche for hiring as many as he needed. She suggested he might want to hire some of the local men as well to tidy the grounds just a bit. All must be perfect for her only daughter's wedding.

The Duke and Duchess of Lamberton rolled into the yard only three days before the wedding. Claire did not even wait for the door to be opened before she burst forth and ran up to where Willa was waiting in her chair. Both women squealed and laughed and cried and hugged.

"Do come into the parlour," Willa said. "We will lock everyone out and have a comfortable coze. I cannot wait to catch up with everything you have done on your wedding trip."

"And I must know about everything which has happened since our marriage," Claire stated. "I cannot believe someone tried to harm you. I know a bit about what you have gone through, and it must have been awful."

Willa did not mince words, "It has not been pleasant, Claire. I have been so afraid, and I still do not feel I am a good choice for a wife to John, but he refuses to listen."

"Good for him. The two of you are meant to be together."

Indeed, the two women did lock themselves in for tea until Fayre finally announced at the door, "Claire, Mama and Papa and the girls have just arrived. The two of you are being selfish holed up in there alone."

The rest of the days flew by in a flurry of excitement and preparations. It was decided that Blythe and her sister together could have served their country better than Wellington himself when it came to drawing up war plans. The men hid out either in the stables or the library. John and Noel caught up on each other's lives by riding. Noel rode John's horse and John rode Pirate. On the eve before the wedding, Willa was unusually quiet. Everyone attributed it to nerves, and it was decided that Claire should speak to her cousin. She found her in Willa's original bedchamber, which Willa had moved back into recently. Entering the room when Willa called for her to come in, Claire first examined the trapeze-like item hanging over the bed.

"Does it work?" she asked Willa.

"Oh, yes. I simply slide the canvas sling beneath me, and then I reach up and grasp the bar. When I pull the rope, it swings me over to my chair, and then I can lower myself into it. John is having another built for our home. Dawson did such a good job on this one that John has hired him to make two more – one for the country home and one for London. Although I do not think I will need them much. John insists we shall be completely unfashionable and share a room once we are married," Willa said with a slight blush.

Claire looked around and then moved to a chair near Willa. "You've been quiet today," she said. "We are all worried about you, but Mama and Aunt Blythe both insist you are only nervous. I have been selected to talk to you about any qualms you may be having about being a bride or about the wedding night."

Willa laughed. "I have grown up around horses, and I think I know the details of what will happen on the wedding night, at least as much as any paralyzed woman can know." She was quiet, wondering if she should confess the real reason behind her mood.

Claire reached ahead to grasp her cousin's and best friend's hand. "Then what is it, Willa? You know you can tell me anything."

Willa sighed and looked out the window she was sitting near. "It's my legs," she whispered. "They have been tingling, and last night I know I was able to move my big toe on my right foot. It wasn't much, more or less a twitch, but usually I try and I can't. This time I tried and I could. Just a bit."

Claire broke into a smile. "That is surely great news," she said.

"Maybe, but please don't say anything to John or my parents. I don't want them to get their hopes up only to have them dashed."

Chapter Seventeen

Stealthy footsteps crept through the kitchen. He had been happy to know the kitchen door had been easy to unlock with the stolen key Nancy had given him shortly before her arrest. The floor was flagstone on the lower level, making little sound as he made his way through the darkness, dragging his hand along the wall until he reached the bottom of the servants' stairs. The steps were stone, which allowed him to access the main floor of the house without incident. From here, his task would become more dangerous. Adjusting the knapsack on his back, he took a deep breath when he reached the landing of the servants' stairs between floors.

Nancy had been detailed, he'd give her that. She had told him to count the steps – one, two, step over three. On the fourth, he was to step to the far right to avoid the squeaky board. Then five, six, seven were fine. On eight he needed to step to the far left and then step over both the ninth and tenth. He was thankful for the solid hand rail as he made the maneuver. Eleven and twelve presented no difficulty. Stepping over thirteen, he made it to the upper landing. There he paused momentarily to get his bearings, for he didn't dare open the wrong door as he had no desire to swing at the end of a rope.

Slowly, as quietly as possible in his stocking feet, for he carried his shoes in the knapsack, he counted the doors on his left. Miss Willa Dutton supposedly slept behind either door number seven or door number eight. This was where the plan was vague. Her original room was eight, but then after the fire had been put out, she had moved to seven with her cousin. The wedding was scheduled for the next day, and the boss lady had assured him she would have moved back into her own room in preparation for her nuptials. If not, however, it might have guests in it. His nerves were making him edgy.

He carefully turned the knob of the door for room number eight, hoping she no longer locked it since he had disappeared from the estate and poor Nancy was locked up awaiting her trial. Yes, he was in luck! The door knob turned and the well-oiled hinges worked, swinging the door wide. Shutting it after himself, he squatted to rummage through the knapsack, digging out the mask and canister he had stolen from a physician. Then he stood, peered through the dark and let his eyes rest on the single form in the bed.

Sliding on his stocking feet, as he felt sure this movement made less noise than a footstep, he made his way to the bed. She lay on her back, brunette hair spread across the pillow, a trapezoid-type lift hanging overhead. Hello, Miss Willa Dutton, he said silently to himself. With the speed of a cat entrapping a mouse he pressed the mask over her nose and mouth, quickly turning on the canister of nitrous oxide with his other hand. Her eyes flew open as she struggled, pushing at the mask. Her strong arms fought, and her hands pulled at his, but he was ready for her. He had pressed the mask to her face with his left hand, leaving his right to capture her small wrists and push her arms down against her midriff. It didn't take long, until her eyes drifted close and her body relaxed. He held the mask down long enough for him to be sure he was safe in removing it, and then he placed it and the canister back in his knapsack, digging out torn strips of cloth that he used to gag her, a piece of rope to bind her wrists. At last, he lifted her upper body and bound her wrists behind her back just to be safe. And then he put the knapsack back on, lifted her body over one shoulder and left the room, being sure to shut the door behind him once again. No reason to offer anyone any clues that she was not in her room.

He wanted to run down the stairs, but he refrained. Again, he carefully counted out the squeaks and steps. Once he arrived at the lowest level of the house, however, he picked up his speed and hurried outside, locking the kitchen door behind himself. Despite the cold dirt and the damp grass, he did not stop to put on his shoes. Instead, he hurried toward the wooded area to the north of the house where he found his horse still patiently waiting and tied up to a tree branch. Throwing Willa's body over the saddle, he did stop long enough to brush off his socks and pull on his shoes. Then swinging up behind Willa's limp form, he directed his horse deeper into the woods.

The boss lady had been worried about the hiding place he had chosen, but he assured her it was the best he could find, that only a few people would even notice it as long as she was properly gagged and chained. She could stay there until she died a slow death from lack of food and water, aided by the falling temperatures at night. He had ridden this way many times, committing the location to memory without ever going in the same direction so as to leave no trail. This night, that was the most important.

His trip took him over a small wooden bridge. Here, he turned his horse to leap the short distance into the stream bed so no hoof prints were noticeable on the far side of the bridge. He smiled as the horse took the jump with nary a hesitation. It had taken him a while to train the beast to perform that. They traversed a good half mile downstream before he tugged the reins, directing his horse to step out of the cold stream and into a marshy area, then eventually onto the grass and toward a copse of trees. There he reined in the horse and got down, tethering the animal to a nearby tree. Picking up Willa's lax body and the knapsack, he carried her into the center of the sheltered area.

The gag was replaced now with a stronger one, one that was tightened so snugly across her face that it would be painful, cutting into the edges of her pretty smile. Then he replaced the ropes that bound her wrists with iron shackles in the front of her body, the kind they used in countries where people were kept in slavery. Kneeling before the hiding place, he rolled her small body down into the hole. Peering in, he saw she had landed on her back. That was good. While her legs might not work, her arms did and he wanted her to have no leverage. Finally, he grabbed the iron stake he had brought. It was a foot and a half long and thick, a good inch to an inch and a half across. He slid it through the ring connecting the wrist shackles to the rusty chain and then pushed it into the ground. Grabbing his hammer, he placed a piece of leather over the end of the stake and then pounded it, over and over, the leather dimming the sound. Even then, each strike of the iron made him grimace, for it seemed the muted sound carried too far in the clear night air.

Satisfied she could not move her upper body, he rose. Using the small spade he had left behind, he filled in the dirt he had previously removed from the bottom side of the fallen tree. There was still a hole there, the size of a badger hole. In fact, he suspected that was the type of animal which had previously lived in the den. She would be able to see a bit of light, enough to fill her heart with both terror and hope. With the den in the close copse and the gag firmly on her mouth, she would not be heard or seen. As her legs did not work, thanks to his somewhat bungled attempt on her life, she could not move them, and her arms were firmly chained down. His work here was clearly done. He left the copse, mounted his horse and rode away.

❧

John awoke with the first signs of the morning dawn. Lying in bed, he smiled and then stretched. Today, he would make Willa his wife. It was what he had been waiting for his entire life. His love, his other half, his future. Martin, with the intuition of an excellent valet, slipped into the room with a cup of coffee. Upon ascertaining that his employer was awake, he walked silently to the bed side, where he fluffed the pillows so John could sit up before wrapping his hands around the warm mug.

"I have ordered hot water, my lord. I thought, perhaps, you would appreciate a bath this morning."

"Remind me to give you a raise, Martin. You are the best valet a man could possibly have."

The other man preened. "Thank you, my lord. It is always my pleasure to serve you."

"Have you already determined what the weather will be to-day?" John asked his man.

"I took the liberty of stepping outside while waiting for Cook to prepare your morning coffee, and I determined it will be a bright and clear day with a slight chill to the air."

"Excellent. It will give me an excuse to wrap my arms around my bride as we ride in the pony trap to the house for the wedding breakfast."

"She will have to drive, then, my lord."

John chuckled. "To tell you the truth, Martin, she is a better driver than I am. And she loves the pony trap — it seems to of-fer her an independence she relishes."

John sipped his coffee; it was strong, just as he liked it. He had been at the Amhearst's so long the cook had learned his likes and dislikes, just as his own cook knew them. "You will attend the wedding, won't you, Martin?"

"I wouldn't miss it for the world, my lord. It isn't every day a man gets to watch his employer marry such a delightful young lady."

"She is delightful, isn't she?"

"Yes, my lord. All of the servants are fond of her. Most have known her since she was a wee girl, but I have grown as fond of her as they all have. It is my belief you could not have chosen a more perfect woman to wed."

The hot water soon arrived, carried in by brawny footmen, and John sank into the tub, letting himself linger until it grew too cold. Meanwhile, Martin aided him in bathing and shaving. At last John rose, towel dried, and then slipped on his dressing gown as Martin reached for the earl's new suit of clothes – his wedding suit.

John dressed with care, working his way through four neck cloths before he got the perfect knot. At last, he stepped into the hallway where he looked toward Willa's room, imagining the flurry of activity that was taking place within. He knew little about a bride's preparation but assumed it, too, started with a bath. Unlike his, however, hers would include scented bath oils which would drive him crazy that night. Molly, Willa's maid, came hurrying up the stairs looking unusually harried. She glanced at him, somewhat wild eyed. John's heart began to beat erratically and his mouth grew dry. Something was wrong.

He stepped closer to her. "What is it, Molly?"

"Miss Willa! I cannot find her."

"What do you mean you cannot find her?" She was restricted to her bed or a wheelchair and could not have gone far.

"When I went into her room, her bed was empty this morning. And her Bath chair is still there beside the bed where she left it last night. I went downstairs to see if she had one of the footmen carry her down, but she is nowhere to be found, and her main floor Bath chair is still sitting in the entry hall."

A feeling of doom settled over him. They had become lax since the disappearance of Jenkins and the arrest of the nurse. "Go find the viscount," he instructed the maid. He turned to a footman who was coming out of another room, "Wake up the Duke of Lamberton," he told him. "Have both of them meet me in the library."

With that, he bounded the stairs and cornered Abbott. "I need to send someone to London posthaste," he told the older man. "Miss Willa is missing, and we must alert Mr. Samuel Parker to return to the estate immediately."

"I will talk to Ward and have him send Brooks. He is a fast rider and can be completely trusted."

Footsteps sounded from above and John looked up to see the viscount and Noel hurrying toward him. He stepped to the library door and swung it open for them to enter.

"What is it?" the viscount inquired. Then, with one look at his future son-in-law's face, he seemed to crumple. "It's Willa isn't it?"

John nodded. "Molly cannot locate her. When the maid went in to wake her, her bed was empty, the chair still beside it. She is not downstairs, nor has the chair here been moved since yesterday evening."

"We must find her," her father said. "Lamberton, would you mind gathering the family and guests?"

"I will do so immediately," the duke replied.

"John, the stable hands trust you. Can you interview them, look around the yard for tracks, and such things? And I'll gather the household servants. Someone must know something."

"I have sent for Mr. Parker, Yale," John spoke. "Abbott said he will send Brooks to town immediately. He said Brooks is fast and trustworthy."

"He is. Brooks would be my choice. Even then, it will take a good day and a half each direction, so we cannot wait for the investigator to arrive."

The men went their separate ways. On the way to the stables, John met Willa's groom, mounted and already headed away at a gallop. The man reined in his horse as he met the earl. "If I see anything along the way which is suspicious, my lord, I will stop at an inn and send word back."

"Please do, Brooks. And ride as fast as you can."

"I will. Ward gave me a fire arm and a generous bag of coins and told me to change horses often and not to delay under any circumstances. I will take the time only for enough sustenance to get me by."

Brooks did not wait for a reply but urged his horse forward and was soon only a small figure on the horizon.

John stepped into the interior of the stable and saw the stable master sitting at his small desk in the office. The man looked up as John approached. He rose from his chair. "Lord Roydon," he greeted John rather glumly. "I hear we have more troubles up at the house."

"Unfortunately, we do. Miss Willa has gone missing. I appreciate you being able to spare Brooks to ride to London,"

"I could not have stopped him. That groom is about as loyal to our Miss Willa as our stable cat is to her newborn kittens."

"I do hope he doesn't run his horse to death in his urgency."

"He won't, but he will change often, and he may run himself to death."

"I was wondering if I could speak to all of the stable hands."

"I thought you might want to. I have already asked Jem to round everyone up and to have them meet us in about a quarter hour in the main stables."

"Thank you, Ward. Have you seen Jenkins anywhere around since he left?"

"Nay, my lord, and if I had, I would have notified the viscount. Although we have no proof he is the one who tampered with the tack and Pirate, we must assume he is, due to his timely disappearance."

Jem appeared in the doorway. "I have everyone gathered a bit early," he announced.

John stood up and flipped the boy a coin, ruffling his hair after the youngster caught it. "Thank ye, me lord," he grinned before running off to sit on the floor of the stable with the grouped men. John walked up to them.

"You may have already heard, but Miss Willa was not in her room when her maid went in to help her prepare for our wedding." There were mumbles and nods of agreement. "I wanted to speak to you to find out if any of you saw or heard anything suspicious. Molly left Miss Willa's bed chamber at about ten in the evening so we can assume someone abducted her after that time."

No one spoke up, they just shook their heads from side to side and looked at each other waiting for any response. One man said "I wish I had." Another said, "I wish I'd been sittin' up with a rifle. Whoever did this deserves to be shot."

John waited for what seemed like an appropriate amount of time and then spoke again. "As Ward stated earlier, we cannot assume Jenkins is the man responsible for the accidents and attempted murders. However, his disappearance, at the same time as the nurse whom we know to be guilty, does seem quite suspicious. Has anyone seen him or heard of him since he left the estate?"

Jem spoke up almost immediately, squirming a bit. "Last Sunday, my uncle over at the next village brought his wagon to pick up ma and my brothers and sisters and me for a rare visit. I swear I saw Jenkins in the inn yard, but I guess I can't be sure. He had his hat pulled low and was facin' the other way. But he stood like Jenkins and he walked like Jenkins."

"That was over in Hedgewater?" John asked.

"Yes, me lord, over at the Cock and Hen."

John offered him a smile. "Thank you, young Jem. That is the only lead we have so far." The boy beamed at him.

It was Ford who said, "If I might make a suggestion, my lord, I think we should divide up and scour the grounds. If she was taken from the house there has to be some footprints or hoof prints in the yard. Jenkins, or whichever scoundrel did this, could nary fly in like a bird."

John heaved a sigh of relief. A loyal staff was worth more than its weight in gold. "We would all appreciate that," he admitted. He turned to the stable master, "Can we use your slate and chalk?" he asked.

"Of course, my lord. I know the estate well. If you don't mind, I'll sketch us out a map and then we can assign men to each section. Jem, you can come with me. Your eyes are much sharper than mine."

John watched as the men gathered around their foreman and then each claimed their plots of land to search. There was much talking about looking for hoof prints, footprints, signs of dragging, marks from wheels, or any signs at all. "Even a wheelbarrow," one man reminded them all.

"I want you all to go in pairs," Ward instructed. "If you find anything which might be a clue, one of you stay with it, the other run up to the house. Where should they go, my lord?"

"To the front door," John answered. "As soon as I return, I will make sure Abbott is posted at the door at all times. The information should be given to me, Lord Amhearst, or my good friend Duke Lamberton."

"Aye, my lord," they all agreed.

At last, John thanked them all and then turned to walk out, pausing at Pirate's stall. He leaned his head against the horses'. "We'll find her, Pirate," he told the steed. "We have to find her."

Back at the house, he found complete chaos. Abbott, always a steady rock, looked as though he had aged ten years. He was actually sitting on a hard straight-backed chair while pandemonium reigned around him. John paused in front of him and, as if the man had only now become aware of him, the butler began to struggle to his feet. John laid a hand on his shoulder.

"Stay seated, Abbott. I need you to be near the door all day. If for any reason you need to leave, please have Morton replace you for that time period. The stable hands are leaving on an extensive search of the grounds and I have instructed them to come to the front door of the house if they should find any clues. I would ask, if that should happen, you notify me, the viscount, or the duke, and keep the stable hand here so that we can talk to him ourselves."

"Yes, my lord, I promise I will follow your instructions to the letter." John could see wetness in the older man's eyes, and as he blinked one tear slid down his cheek. John knew how the butler felt; he wanted to cry as well, but taking action was more important.

He turned toward the library and could hear sobbing coming from the parlour. His best friend's new wife appeared in the door. "What are we doing to find her?" Claire demanded. He remembered the adversities the duchess had undergone last spring in London and knew her to be a strong woman. So was his Willa, and now that was more important than anything. She had to be strong, and she had to be alive.

"The stable hands are already searching the grounds," he replied. "As soon as I have spoken to your uncle and Noel, I will leave to search."

Claire crossed her arms around her waist, hugging herself. "Papa is in the library with them. He is praying."

Claire's father was a man of God. "That may be the most important thing we can do," John admitted.

Entering the library, he asked for an update and noted that, indeed, the good reverend was on his knees before the hearth, hands folded in quiet prayer.

"Edward," his brother-in-law said of that man, "has offered to ride into the village to alert the vicar the wedding will have to be delayed once again. He will then ask the vicar's aid in alerting the people of the village, interviewing them, and asking for any assistance they can offer."

Edward had risen and turned to the group of men. "Thank you," John told him.

"And I thought to ride throughout the surrounding roads and speak to the neighbors. I will look for anything which seems suspicious and will ask anyone I meet if they know anything," the duke said.

"Particularly ask about a groom named Jenkins who disappeared some while ago after the nurse was taken to prison for attempting to kill Willa. We suspect him of tampering with the tack and trying to poison her horse."

Noel nodded. "I will do so."

John turned to the viscount, "Yale, I believe you should stay here. Ward has sent all of his stable hands out in pairs to search the estate. If they should find even the smallest clue, they are to divide up, one staying at the site and the other returning here to speak to you. I have asked Abbott to stay at the front door at all times only to be replaced by Morton for his brief respites, in case someone comes to the door to speak to you."

Yale nodded. "And you?" he asked John.

"Young Jem went to Hedgewater with his family last Sunday to visit an uncle. Although he cannot be sure, he believes he may have seen Jenkins in the yard of the Cock and Hen. I plan on riding there to make inquiries. If Jenkins is there, I will attempt to not kill the man so that I might find out where my Willa is. I also believe we all should take a page out of Edward's book as well and pray with all our might."

Chapter Eighteen

Willa woke up groggy. Indeed, her eyes just didn't seem to want to stay open. She kept drifting off to sleep and then waking up again. Finally, she came to enough to realize something was wrong. Her legs tingled horribly, and her arms were uncomfortable and stretched over her head. There was something in her mouth and it was hurting her face, cutting into the edges of her mouth. Trying to move her arms, she realized she could not and then discovered her wrists were manacled and her arms chained to something. Wherever she was, it was dark with only the smallest glimmer of light slightly above her and to the right. She tried to scream for help, but with the fabric cutting into her mouth, she could do no more than utter a slight squeak. Panic began to set in.

Stop it! she commanded herself, for she needed to stay calm and evaluate the situation. Breathing deeply through her nose, she tried to compose herself. The thing she was most aware of was the tingling in her legs, an incredible desire to move them. She tried to and was jubilant when she realized she could – maybe not a lot, but she could move both legs slightly to the left and right. Willa realized she wasn't paralyzed. It was a miracle: she was healing!

She thought, but wasn't sure, she was still in her nightgown. Reaching her tongue out she realized she was gagged with strips of rough fabric. The gag was extremely tight. Wiggling her fingers she discovered there was iron shackled on both wrists with a chain fastening them together, allowing only about a foot of movement between her hands. Willa could move them closer together and reach her fingers down enough to realize she was in a dirt hole, perhaps a grave of some kind. Moving her hands to the middle, she discovered a thick stake was pounded into the ground through a ring in the chain.

Fighting off the continued grogginess and her fear, Willa remembered that today was her wedding day. In fact, she was to be married at ten o'clock in the morning. As her eyes became accustomed to the darkness, she looked toward the bit of light. It was a hole, maybe big enough for an animal to crawl through. Above her there was something big and dark which lay across the entire hole in the ground. Concentrating on it, she decided it was a tree and that is when she recognized where she was at. Once when riding Pirate through the woods to the north of the estate, she had come upon the prettiest little copse of trees, and she had dismounted in order to explore it, wondering what lay inside. Brooks had waited patiently outside of the copse for her. What she had discovered was a big fallen tree trunk — an oak, with a grave sized hole underneath. When she emerged and told Brooks about it, he told her she shouldn't have looked inside for it sounded like a badger's den and those animals were vicious. "It might have been a den at one time, Brooks," she had said, "but it has long since been abandoned."

Willa was thirsty and tried to suck on her cheeks and tongue enough to work up some saliva. With the gag in her mouth, it was next to impossible. She tried to remember what had happened, and that's when she remembered waking up as some sort of rubbery mask had been held over her mouth. She had fought it, but a strong hand had restrained her wrists. Looking up into the eyes of her assailant, she had recognized Jenkins just before she had succumbed to unconsciousness.

Moving her legs again, she realized they were weak, but she knew she could make them work enough to move a short distance. Thinking of the copse, she knew as soon as Molly found her room empty they would all be out looking for her. They would look in homes and barns and empty buildings. But it dawned on her that the chances of them looking in a badger den in the middle of the copse were slim to none. If she was going to live to marry the man she loved – and now that she knew she would probably walk again, she could not wait to marry him–she would have to rescue herself.

Letting her eyes drift shut for just a moment, she thought about the situation. She needed to keep moving her legs, to strengthen them enough she could walk or crawl or stand on them. Then she also had to get free. If the stake was pounded only into the dirt that felt damp beneath her, she could work it free. Willa had been paralyzed and lifting herself and pushing a chair. No doubt her upper body strength was highly developed, compared to most other women of her station. Forcing her eyes open, she wrapped both hands around the stake and began to push and pull. First she went back and forth, then she went side to side. Thinking about rowing on a pleasant, placid lake, dipping the oars beneath the surface, pulling towards her, and lifting them out, she worked on. Visualizing birds singing, merrily in the trees on the bank, John's face smiling upon her, teasing her about being so independent kept her going. Imagining John telling her how much he loved her caused her to push away her fear.

John rode into the Cock and Hen, reining his horse in from a gallop to a full stop in a cloud of dust. He saw no one outside, so he tied up his horse and walked quickly into the inn. The innkeeper set down the tankard he was polishing and looked up at him. "May I help you, sir?"

Striding across to the bar, John laid a gold coin on the gleaming wooden bar top. "I'm looking for someone by the name of Will Jenkins. He used to work as a stable hand for Lord Amhearst near the next village over. Someone told me they thought they saw him in the inn yard not more than a few days ago."

The man picked up the coin and pocketed it. "Yes, sir, he has been staying here — out in the stable loft. Can't say I know much about 'im nor think much of 'im, but he ain't caused no trouble yet."

"Do you mind if I go look for him?"

"No sir, but you won't find 'im. Rides off every day to the south, toward Stonybridge."

Stonybridge was a mid-sized town which had much more to offer than the smaller villages. It was not a long distance away, but it was far enough he would need to pace his horse if he was going to continue to ride him.

"My wife is just pulling a fresh-baked meat pie out of the oven. It's mid-day and I could quickly serve you a piece with a tankard before you make your way on down the road."

John could think of nothing other than finding Willa, but he was sensible enough to know his horse needed to rest. "Why don't you do that? If you don't mind I'll slip out and water my horse before I eat."

"Robert," the man bellowed, and a teenaged boy emerged from the back immediately. "Go water this man's horse, would you? I suspect he's been running hard. Mebbe give 'im a scoop o' oats."

"Yes, Pa," the boy said while looking out the window. "I guess he's the buckskin?"

"He is," John affirmed.

"Fine lookin' piece o' horseflesh. Be happy to." And then he was out the door in a flash.

John took a seat on one of the stools. "That boy o' mine has an eye for the horses, he does," the innkeeper said as he set a fresh ale in front of the earl. As John lifted it to take a healthy draw, he suddenly realized how thirsty he was. The innkeeper called behind him, "Martha, is the pie ready? If it is, we could use a hearty slice of it out here."

A plump and cheerful looking woman appeared momentarily with a pottery plate holding a good-sized piece of meat pie, thick gravy running out from either side. She had a towel wrapped around the edge of the plate and as she set it in front of him she said, "Now you be careful, sir. I've had the plate warming in the oven."

John took a bite of the pie, chewed, enjoyed, and swallowed it. He would have to ride onto Stonybridge. It would be drawing near evening when he arrived, and he might have to put up at an inn there to have time to make inquiries. Knowing he needed to let Yale know what his plan was so they wouldn't worry about him, he looked up at the other man. "I need to get a message to Lord Amhearst over at Leedsville. Do you think your son could deliver it for me yet today?"

"Aye, he could and would be happy to. Would you like pen and paper to write it out?"

"Please." Soon John had what he needed to prepare the note. It was simple, telling Yale only that he had another lead on Jenkins and he might not be back until the morrow. By the time he had finished and sealed it with wax impressed with his signet ring, the boy had just returned. "Your horse has been watered and is finishing off his oats," he said.

The innkeeper said, "This fine gentleman needs a note delivered to Lord Amhearst near Leedsville. I told him you would be happy to deliver it."

The boy smiled broadly. "I will, sir. I have only to fetch my coat and I can be off. Should I take the roan, Pa?"

After man and son had discussed which horse the boy should take and he checked with John on his instructions, the boy was ready to leave, and John watched through the window as the lad galloped out of the inn yard. John had paid the boy and given his father some for his efforts as well. He now stood and paid for his meal.

"If you don't mind me askin'," the innkeeper spoke, "what are you needing Jenkins fer?"

John thought about it and decided not to mince his words. "I'm thinking he may be involved in the abduction of my fiancée.

"And what might that young lady's name be?"

"Viscount Amhearst's daughter, Miss Willa Dutton."

"I'll ask around fer you, and if I hear anything I'll send my son to Lord Amhearst's with a message."

"I appreciate it," John said as he walked out the door, finding his horse resting in a stall in the stables. He mounted and turned toward Stonybridge.

The ride to that town took little more than an hour at the pace he set. When he arrived, he boarded his horse at a stables where he made an inquiry about Jenkins. Learning nothing, he walked to the nearest public house where he had more luck. Although the name brought no recognition, the barkeep recognized his description. He had little more information than that, though, and John gained no more useful knowledge in the next few establishments he stopped at. As dark drew nigh, he stepped into a hotel to see if they had a room. He did not have a change of clothes with him, but washing off the dirt from the road would be a welcome move, even if he had to put his dirty clothes back on.

He was, indeed, able to procure a room for the night. Requesting hot water, John washed up as best he could without stripping. Then he went down to the dining room to get some dinner. Again, he wasn't hungry, but he reminded himself he had to keep up his strength for Willa. Indeed, he had to think positively, could not think she had been killed, had to believe she was somewhere, scared and hungry, but not injured. He ordered a beef steak and potato, finished it, and washed it down with a good wine. As he was rising to go back to his room, he suddenly felt a strong sense of foreboding. Even before he had turned around, he knew no good came from what he was about to face.

"Why, if it isn't Lord Roydon," the female voice said.

Turning around, he looked directly into the face of smug evil, slightly more twisted than the last time he had set his gaze upon it. "Lady Regina Norton," he stated coldly.

❦

Willa was nearing exhaustion but continued to push herself. It was almost dark, she could see from the hole. She would continue to work until it was completely dark, and then, and only then, would she allow herself to sleep for a while.

Her legs were much improved. The tingling was fading away and she had been able to lift her knees several inches off the ground. She had rotated her feet and moved her legs often. Oh, they were so weak!

Moving the stake back and forth had caused her arms to scream in pain, but the dirt around it had loosened. While she was not yet able to pull the stake out, she would be able to – she knew she would with time.

A rumbling in her stomach made her wish for food. Once again, she sucked on her tongue and the inside of her mouth to dredge up a bit of saliva. She longed for a cup of tea, a perfectly brewed cup of refreshing tea. When she escaped, she reminded herself, she could have all the tea she wanted. Furthermore, she could marry John, have babies, and ride Pirate.

The mere thought of what awaited her urged her on, and she continued to work at removing the stake, even past dark.

❦

John looked at the woman who had tortured the Duchess of Lamberton with a blackmail scheme. His father had, at one time, suggested Lady Norton as a possible wife for him, and after meeting her several times last spring, he could not abide the thought. Her scheme had not ended well for her. She had been with child; the father was a wastrel and a scoundrel. Lady Norton's brother had been killed by Noel after he had tried a second time to attack Claire. Lady Norton had been sent to Yorkshire to live with an aunt. He brought this up now.

"I heard you were in Yorkshire with your aunt." John had a sinking feeling she had something to do with Willa's disappearance. When she didn't reply, he went on. "Stonybridge seems like a rather odd location in which to meet you."

"I'm visiting someone," she said then.

"His name wouldn't be Will Jenkins, would it?" John had decided on a direct attack. He noted a flicker of surprise in her eyes.

"I've never heard that name." She went on. "I might say Stonybridge is an unusual town in which to meet you, Lord Roydon. Why are you here?"

"My fiancée, Miss Willa Dutton, is missing. I am looking for her, and a tip led me here."

"Oh, too bad," she murmured in an unsympathetic voice. "When is the wedding?"

John unclenched his jaw long enough to answer. "It was scheduled for this morning."

"How sad. Did she, perhaps, change her mind and not want to tell you?"

"I don't believe so. I'm sure someone, perhaps two or three people, played a part in abducting her."

"Well, we will hope it is not too late when you find her. Of course, if it is, I'm sure there are any number of women who would be willing to make you a happy man. Why, do you remember that our fathers had at one time hoped for us to marry?"

"I do remember, and I cannot express how thankful I am we each met someone else more to our liking." He paused. "By the way, I heard you were with child. Baron Sully's wasn't it?"

"I lost the child," she admitted. "It's just as well. It turns out that Baron Sully didn't envision himself as a married man." She looked up. Fiddling with her reticule, she went on, "I am afraid I must say farewell. It is time I retire to my room."

John needed to know where her room was, and she didn't appear to have a maid with her. "Perhaps I should escort you to your room, Lady Norton. I do not see that you have a maid with you."

"Oh, I did not require a maid to accompany me to dinner. Likewise, I will be fine on my way to my room." She turned and practically fled. John followed her, acting as though he were going to his own room. He was able to see which room she was in – 204. Luck was with him as his room was next door to hers. John held back until she had shut the door to hers and then he went into his, locking the door behind him. Telling himself he would sleep lightly and try to rise at the first sound of noise from next door, he laid down on the bed fully dressed. If she went anywhere, he intended to follow her.

The sounds of movement came surprisingly early for a member of the ton. John got up at the first sounds and was alert within minutes. He craved a cup of coffee, but skipped it. Instead, he cracked open his room door a small amount and then leaned against the wall where he could tell if she or anyone left the room.

Patience paid off. Lady Norton left her room alone dressed in a cape and bonnet. He let her get a head start, and he left his room when she was halfway down the stairs. Exiting the hotel, he saw her go down the walkway to his left. John followed her, dodging into doorways whenever she paused. Twice she looked back, and he prayed that she had not seen him. She stepped into the doorway of a dark and shadowy stable. That was when he saw Jenkins. Lady Norton and Jenkins were in hushed conversation. Upset that he couldn't get close enough to hear the words, John crouched below a fence just in time for her to pass him when Lady Norton whirled and rushed out of the stables. He thought about following, but then he made the decision to stay with Jenkins. Soon, he decided he had made the right choice when Jenkins led a horse out of the stables, mounted him in front of the building, and then rode away the same direction John had ridden in from.

John ran to the stables where his horse was, thankful he had paid the man the night before and asked he leave the horse saddled. He swung up on his own horse and followed Jenkins. It took some hard riding to keep Jenkins in his sight. In fact, there were several times he thought he had lost him, but then eventually he would catch up with him again. They were halfway between Hedgewater and Leedsville and John's horse was slowing. Indeed, John had ridden the beast hard, too hard. Ahead was a curve, and John knew that past it was a bridge which crossed a good sized stream. Pushing his horse more, he knew Willa must be alive. If they had killed her, there would be no reason for any association between Jenkins and Lady Norton, nor would Jenkins have ridden off as though he were on a mission.

As John rounded the curve, he saw no sign of Jenkins. There were no distinct hoof prints, no dust rising from the road. It was as though the man had simply disappeared. John reined in his horse and looked up and down the stream. The bridge had no railing, but there were a few places where a man on a horse could have ridden around and into the stream. He dismounted, searching for tracks. There was nothing. John's heart sank, and a cold despair set into his soul. He had lost the man. What if he was on his way to kill Willa?

It was full daylight, and Willa was working on loosening the stake. She had slept a bit, fitfully of course, but still she had gotten some rest. The tingling had completely left her legs, and she could move them. They were weak, and she wasn't sure she would be able to stand, but she thought she could crawl, and that might be enough. As she lay there moving the stake to and fro, side to side, she suddenly heard noises that were different from the normal sounds of the woods. All she had previously been able to hear had been birds and the scurrying associated with small animals. In fact, one time she had seen a rabbit hop by the opening.

She continued to work on the stake, but otherwise lay silently, listening. She didn't know whether to try to scream to draw attention to herself or to be silent and play dead in case

Jenkins or someone else came to kill her. In the end, she decided to scream. If it was someone who meant her harm, that person already knew where she was. It made more sense to let her presence be known in case it was a rescuer.

The gag made it hard, if not impossible, to scream, but she worked up everything she had and let it go. What emerged was a form of a scream, not loud, but in the quiet of the woods it might be enough to be heard.

Suddenly, the dirt began to disappear from the edge of the hole, revealing a shovel and a pair of boots. A man's boots. She didn't think the person was there to help her, or surely he would have stuck a head in to say something like "Hello, stay calm, we'll get you out soon." Instead, there was nothing except for the shoveling which caused dirt to skitter down and land on her. She worked on the stake more frantically.

The shoveling stopped. Jenkins' face appeared in the opening. "Why, hello there, Miss Dutton," he said with an evil sneer to his voice. "I thought you might like to know your fiancé has been out searching for you."

Willa lay still.

"Too bad you'll be dead by the time he finds you. The boss lady, she says I have to kill you."

Willa had to know who it was. She tried to say "who?" but the sound came out more like the hoot of an owl.

"Who is the boss lady? Is that what you want to know? I guess it won't hurt to say. After all, dead folks can't talk, so who would you tell?"

Lady Regina Norton, he told her. Willa realized Lady Norton was insane, just like her brother. She had to be. Willa watched as Jenkins reached into the hole with a sharp knife aimed toward her neck. "I gotta slit your throat, luv. A bullet would be more humane-like, but it would make too much noise, and I don't intend to hang for your death."

Willa squirmed and jerked her hands up as hard as she could. The stake came out of the ground with a force she had not expected. She brought it down across his arms. He dropped the knife and howled in pain. She raised the stake again and brought it down on his head as hard as she could. His body slumped immediately. Not knowing whether or not she had killed him, and certainly not caring, Willa took a deep breath and then began her escape.

It was a struggle, to be sure. Her legs were weak, and her hands shackled. Not taking the time to remove the gag, Willa pounded the stake into the ground at the edge of the hole and pulled with all her might until her weak legs were bent beneath her. Pushing the limp body of her attacker aside, she moved the stake and jabbed it into the ground a bit ahead. Then she pulled once again. A foot at a time, she managed to drag herself out of the hole. Sparing not a glance for Jenkins, she got up on her knees in much the same way an infant first crawls, and she started her trip to safety. Willa jabbed the stake into the ground, pulling herself with her arms while pushing her knees forward. Then she started all over again. She was on her way to her love.

Chapter Nineteen

John rode onto the Amhearst estate in the most dejected mood he had ever experienced. As soon as he reached the door, a groom ran from the stable and took his horse's reins to allow John to dismount. "Take good care of him," John requested. "He's exhausted from a hard ride." He patted his horse on the neck and walked to the door, where he was met by Yale and Noel. Without asking, he could see the questions in their eyes, and with anguish in his voice, he said, "I had Jenkins. I was following him until the big curve between the village and Hedgewater. My horse was getting tired and I could barely keep up. I lost him there. It's like he just disappeared on the bridge. There weren't any prints going down into the stream. I don't know if he got so far ahead of me I lost him or what."

Yale set his hand on his shoulder. "You did what you could, and you know more than we were able to learn. We haven't found or heard anything."

"It's Lady Regina Norton," John told them, looking up specifically at Noel. "She was in Stonybridge at a hotel. It was the same place I stayed, and I followed her the next morning to a run-down stable where she met with Jenkins. I could only follow one of them, and I believe she was going back to the hotel, so I chose to follow Jenkins instead."

"It was the right choice," Noel said. "I wonder why Lady Norton is trying to kill Willa."

"I don't know. It doesn't make much sense except she told me that if I were free there would be any number of women willing to marry me. Then she reminded me how our fathers had wanted us to marry at one time."

Yale looked at him in bewilderment. After a moment he continued. "You need to rest, son. You're practically weaving on your feet."

It was at that moment young Jem, the tack boy, ran up to them. "I heard a horse in the woods," he said breathless and excited. "I was out to check the feed in the north paddock and I heard a horse neigh. Ain't nobody goes out there, but Miss Willa and Brooks on their rides."

All three men looked up sharply. "Saddle Pirate for me, will you, Jem? My horse is worn out." John asked. Yale and Noel almost simultaneously said, "And have our horses saddled as well."

Abbott had been loitering in the doorway. Yale turned to him. "Tell Edward to stay with the women and that we're going out again.

Not more than a quarter hour later, the three armed men and a handful of grooms, including young Jem, rode toward the woods.

※

Willa looked over her shoulder at the progress she had made. She sighed. This was slow going. Her knees ached; she knew they were bloody and injured. Her hands had blisters on them from the stake, yet she continued to slam it into the ground. Each time she drug herself forward, her arm muscles screamed in pain, and her leg muscles were so tired and weak they quivered.

She had gotten the gag off her mouth. Unable to loosen the knot, she had simply pulled it down around her neck. Willa's stomach growled in hunger, and she was so thirsty she had actually tried licking some dampness off the grass in a shaded area. Maybe in another hour she could scream for help. At this point, it would be wasted breath as she wasn't close enough to the estate to be heard. Her mouth was so dry she didn't believe she should waste her screams, for she was sure they were limited without water.

Then she heard it – a thrashing through the undergrowth of the woods. She had opened her mouth to scream when she heard a feminine voice softly call. "Jenkins, where are you? Did you kill her yet?"

The voice sounded familiar to Willa. It wasn't Nancy, however, and Willa looked around frantically for a place to hide. She had just located a bush and was crawling toward it when Lady Regina Norton on a horse broke into the clearing.

"Why, there you are, Miss Dutton. Where is Jenkins?"

The woman was brandishing a gun and slid rather awkwardly off her horse, dropping the reins to the ground. Willa screamed. She had no time to waste, for there was a crazed look in Lady Norton's eyes.

"I killed Jenkins," she announced baldly, her voice hoarse, although she couldn't be sure she had and would just as soon let the court system deal with him.

"I should have known better than to hire him. Both he and that nurse were worthless. You should be dead many times over by now."

"Why?" Willa asked, sure she probably would die and wanting to know the reason for Lady Norton's actions.

"You're engaged to the earl and about to marry. I can't let that happen. I want to marry him."

Willa laughed. "He wouldn't marry you if you were the last woman on earth. You're ruined, rude, and demented. Even if you kill me, even if John marries, it would be to someone else and not to you."

"But I hate Yorkshire. I hate my life."

"You should have thought about that a while ago." Then Willa realized she was not offering the other woman any hope and that would definitely get her killed. "It's not too late. You can change your life, improve your reputation, and become a better person."

"Ha. That is never going to happen. Society no longer accepts me, my father doesn't even care about me. He hasn't come to visit and I haven't seen him in months."

"He's your father, and he surely loves you." Keep her talking, Willa thought. Hopefully, she was close enough to the estate for her scream to have been heard. People would be looking for her, of that she was sure. John would be searching for her around the clock.

"My father only loved my wastrel of a brother, and since the Duke killed him, he cares about nothing other than the bottle. For that matter, he hasn't cared about anything else for a long time."

"How sad," Willa commented, and then as Lady Norton raised the gun, Willa screamed again and began to crawl away. The madwoman could shoot her, but Willa decided it would be in the back. She would not sit still to die.

❧

A scream resounded through the air, and John, waiting for no one to follow him, nudged Pirate in the flank. That horse needed no further urging. John would swear he knew his owner's scream, for he suddenly started pounding through the woods, leaping over fallen logs and undergrowth. John was an excellent rider, and it was all he could do to stay atop the beast. He was aware that they were leaving the others behind.

The horse's hooves rose into the air again, although John was sure they had barely touched the ground since Willa had screamed. He clung to the saddle as Pirate soared over a tall bush and landed gracefully in a clearing where the scene almost caused John's heart to stop. Willa was crawling, her wrists shackled to a stake she was using to pound into the ground and pull herself along. Lady Regina Norton stood with a gun aimed at the back of Willa's head. Only his fiancée's strange bobbing movement kept her from being in the site of the gun.

Pirate reared and lost John. Never in his life had he been dumped onto the ground on his back. He saw the stallion pawing at the air, and a whinny that sounded like a call of war emitted from his lungs. Lady Norton was within feet of the horse and his pawing hooves. The woman raised the gun to shoot Pirate, and Willa screamed, "No."

John, feeling completely helpless, scrambled up to run to Willa, keeping his eye on Lady Norton. And then it happened. Pirate started to drop to the ground, but one hoof made contact with the top of Lady Regina's head. The woman crumpled to the ground. John dropped down next to Willa and scooped her up. Tears slid down his face. "I love you, Willa. Sweetheart, I love you so much." His voice was choked with emotion. He clutched her to his chest and rocked her back and forth then raised a hand to gently stroke around the edges of her mouth, where the gag had chaffed her tender skin.

The others broke into the clearing. Yale leaped from his horse and ran to Willa and John, dropping down to pull the two of them into a hug. "You're safe," he uttered. "Thank God you're safe."

Noel walked over to Lady Norton's quiet form and squatted next to her, laying his fingers on the side of her neck. "She's gone," he announced.

Willa struggled to sit up and look over. "Pirate killed her." Then she looked at John and her father. "You might like to know, I can move my legs!"

"I saw that," John replied. "You can crawl."

"Yes, they're weak, but I will walk down the aisle at our wedding. Now, please take me home. I need a cup of tea."

John chuckled, the relief of finding his love alive causing it to burst forth more heartily than he would have expected. He stood up and scooped her into his arms, whistling at Pirate who immediately pranced to their sides.

Willa had snuggled up against his chest but now lifted her head to look at them. She pointed toward the east. "Back in there a ways is a little copse. Inside of it is a fallen log. I was held in a hole under the log, and that is where Jenkins' body is. I hit him over the head with the stake, and I don't know if he's dead or alive."

Noel looked at John and Yale. "Why don't the two of you take Willa home? The men and I will take care of things here."

Willa's homecoming would be remembered by everyone for years to come and whispered about by servants below stairs for just as long. When Yale and John rode in astride the horses, Willa was clutched firmly to John's chest as though he would never let her go. The household heard the news via Abbott, who forgot his butler's manners with a hearty yell which carried through the house. "She's alive, and she's home!"

Footmen emerged from the inner rooms of the house and hurried down to assist. Morton wiped at his eyes as he rushed to Pirate's side, "Here, my lord, I'll take her." He held out his arms and took Willa into his as John reluctantly handed her down. Other footmen took the horse's reins as the grooms were still out at the scene of the crime.

"We'll take the horses over to the stable, my lords," one said. "I think two of the older stable hands are still here."

John would have reached for Willa again, but she stopped him. "Morton, please set me on my feet. I think I can walk with your support. At least I would like to try."

The women and Edward had appeared on the step. "You can walk again, Willa?" her mother exclaimed as she lifted her skirts and ran to her daughter's side.

"I think so," Willa said from within an embrace. "My legs are weak, though."

Morton gently set her on the ground but didn't release her. Willa's knees began to fold, but then she caught herself and rose back up to stand.

John slipped to Willa's side and slid his arm boldly around her waist. He smiled down at her. "Do you want to try to walk?"

"Yes," she said.

Then, as Yale took Morton's place on her other side, he said to Morton, "Run out and get Dawson for us, Morton. We need to get these manacles and chains off Miss Willa.

Needing no other instruction, the young footman hurried away.

Willa took a deep breath and determinedly moved one foot in front of the other. Her legs were shaky, but they held her up. She laughed with pure joy. "If you can give me a day or two, John, I will walk down the aisle to you at our wedding. Of course, it's a good thing the village church is small," she said with a laugh.

John pulled her gently closer to him and kissed her despite her father standing next to them. The viscount discreetly averted his eyes. Clapping erupted in front of the house and when they looked up, all of the servants and family were applauding.

By the time she had taken the dozen steps to the house, Willa was exhausted. "I believe I will let you carry me in, John. Or are you too tired?"

"I will never be too tired for that," he replied. "Although I suspect I look pretty haggard." He swung her up into his arms and asked, "Where to?"

"The parlour until I get these chains off. I want a cup of tea and something to eat."

Abbott looked at a footman and said, "Tea for Miss Willa. And tell Cook to make it fast." Then the man hurried ahead to open the door to the parlour, fluffing the cushions on the settee. As John set Willa down on it, stretching her legs out, the butler fussed over her, adjusting the pillows more for her comfort.

Dawson appeared in the doorway, looking uncomfortable in the luxurious surroundings of the house. He had a large block of wood, a chisel, and a hammer. He approached quietly and smiled at Willa. "Why, Miss Willa, it looks like you got yourself in quite a fix," he said, his deep voice echoing in the room.

"I did, Dawson," she retorted. "I'm hoping you can get me out of it."

John, who had perched on a footstool at Willa's side, stood up, albeit wearily. "Here, Dawson, I think you need this stool."

"I'll kneel, my lord. I'm afraid I'll get the stool dirty."

"You go right ahead," Blythe said as she scurried closer. "I've been wanting to have it recovered anyway."

And so Dawson eased himself onto the footstool, put his wood block down and then gently laid Willa's wrist on top of it. He positioned the chisel and then looked at her. "Now, Miss Willa, I don't want to hurt you, so please try to hold still. Just a couple of strikes with this big hammer, and we'll have these off of you."

The ringing of the iron hammer striking the chisel against the locks on the manacles made the family members cringe, but surprisingly soon, one wrist was free and Dawson had placed the other on the wood block. As Morton and a maid carried in a tea tray, Dawson got up and left with the stake, chain, and manacles in his hand. It was as Blythe poured tea and filled a plate with all kinds of delicacies when they all turned to Willa expectantly.

John took his seat on the stool again and let his eyes gaze on Willa's face. She smiled and then patted his cheek. "She was trying to kill me so she could have you, my love."

John snorted despite the company. "I would never look twice at her."

"That's what I told her, but I think insanity runs in their family."

"No doubt, if she could possibly believe I would ever marry anyone if I could not marry you." Then he looked up at the crowd of people in the room. After a moment he turned his head to look over his shoulder to the window and said, "Do you all see that unusual bird out the window?" As everyone looked, he leaned forward and kissed Willa lingeringly. In the background, there was a collective sigh and one or two feminine giggles.

Later, Willa had been carried upstairs to enjoy a hot bath and to have her poor knees bandaged and to be checked over by Dr. Saunders. John joined his soon to be father-in-law, his best friend, and Willa's uncle in the library. Brandy had been served all around and they were all comfortably seated when Noel said, "I think we have cleaned everything up. One of the grooms is taking Lady Norton's body to her father. Jenkins was alive but will awake with a fierce headache in Newgate Prison."

"Willa said they put her in a badger den under a fallen tree in the center of the copse and then chained her down with the stake, no doubt planning to leave her to die," John's voice was filled with anger. "But she had worked on the stake, moving it back and forth until she loosened it because he had made the mistake of pulling her arms over her head where she could grasp it. I guess she knew the night before that she might be getting her feeling back in her legs because they had begun to tingle," he recounted.

"That's what she told Claire," the duke said, "but she asked Claire not say anything until she knew for sure so she would not get anyone's hopes up."

There was a knock at the library door, and Abbott announced the physician. Dr. Saunders was welcomed into the room.

"I am happy, nay ecstatic, to announce Miss Dutton has come to no real harm. Her knees will be sore for a while, as well as the palms of her hands where she has a number of blisters. But overall, she is in excellent health. And that telling tiny jerk of her foot right after her accident was, indeed, a good sign. Sometimes a person can suffer such an injury that, instead of leaving the spine permanently damaged, the tissues surrounding the spine can swell. When this happens paralysis sets in due to the pressure on the nerves, but with time, if the swelling is reduced, the patient can regain feeling and motion."

"So as the swelling went down," John put in, "the tingling in her lower extremities began just like when one sleeps on an arm for too long."

"Exactly," the physician said. "Of course, her legs are weak as she hasn't used them in such a while, but she's strong and determined, so she will soon be back to her old self."

"So we can reschedule the wedding?" the viscount asked.

"Please," John replied, "and let's make it soon."

t

The wedding was three days hence. The bells tolled in the little village and everyone who could escape from their work crowded into the small church. Those who did not fit filled the churchyard awaiting a glimpse of the bride and groom.

Willa, whose legs were still not quite back to normal, supported herself on her father's arm as Fayre began playing the organ. Tentatively, Willa took a step and then another, guided by John's loving countenance at the altar. Claire led the way, and the duke stood to John's left smiling upon his own wife. As Yale handed his only daughter off to the Earl of Roydon, he smiled, although he wiped away a few tears that spilled down his cheek.

Willa's uncle and the local vicar were sharing the wedding ceremony, and just before they began, John leaned down and winked at her saying, "Sweetheart, you'll never release me now!"

The End

About the Author

Ilene Withers grew up in western Nebraska in a town with a population of four, and later, on a cattle ranch. After high school, she attended college long enough to meet the love of her life. In the ensuing years, she had a daughter and moved from Nebraska to Texas, to New Mexico, and then on to Colorado. Eventually, she decided to go back to college and finish her degree. She graduated with a BA in English Writing in 2012.

Ilene started writing a community news column for a very small county paper in high school. Later, she wrote a mental health column for another small newspaper. What she loved writing the most, however, was holiday plays for her sister's one room country school programs featuring western and historical themes such as mail order brides and stagecoach stops. Finally, she wrote her first romance novel on a portable typewriter while living in West Texas. While that manuscript has never left her desk drawer, she later took a week off of work and wrote her debut novel, *The Blackmailed Beauty*. After much rewriting and fine tuning, that manuscript was published by Astraea Press in October 2013. *To Release an Earl* is her second Regency romance and a sequel to her debut novel.

Ilene is a member of Romance Writers of America, Colorado Romance Writers, and the Beau Monde. She lives in Loveland, Colorado with her musician husband and her Maine Coon cat.

Clean Reads

ALL STORY. NO GUILT.

CPSIA information can be obtained
at www.ICGtesting.com
Printed in the USA
FSOW01n1213280316
18517FS

9 781621 354772